S0-BUC-365

Dear Reader,

This is a special book to me for a number of reasons, not the least of which is that it is my 50th book for Silhouette. My association with Silhouette has been a long and, I trust, mutually satisfying one, but it is my relationship with my readers that keeps me coming back to the keyboard day after day with new stories to tell. Your patronage and input are greatly appreciated. It has been the best of all possible worlds for me, so much so that I simply cannot imagine another more satisfying, and it is you, dearest reader, who makes it possible. I thank God for each and every one of you and the opportunity to continue doing what I so love to do. It is my fervent hope that you will enjoy this story of overcoming grief and disappointment by learning to live and love again. Those of us who have suffered such losses—and haven't we all?—know that life has a way of pulling us back into the fray even when we feel too wounded to soldier on, but that it is love which makes the battle worthwhile and the victory sweet.

I wish you love, therefore, to see you through whatever dark hour may come, and faith in the joy which must surely follow. Most important, I thank you for picking up this book and thereby becoming no small part of my own ongoing delight. To the editors at Silhouette, most especially to those with whom I have worked closely, I express my deep gratitude for the many years of support and guidance.

God bless,

Arlene James

Dear Reader,

I'm dreaming of summer vacations—of sitting by the beach, dangling my feet in a lake, walking on a mountain or curling up in a hammock. And in each vision, I have a Silhouette Romance novel, and I'm happy. Why don't you grab a couple and join me? And in each book take a look at our Silhouette Makes You a Star contest!

We've got some terrific titles in store for you this month. Longtime favorite author Cathie Linz has developed some delightful stories with U.S. Marine heroes and *Stranded with the Sergeant* is appealing and fun. Cara Colter has the second of her THE WEDDING LEGACY titles for you. *The Heiress Takes a Husband* features a rich young woman who's struggling to prove herself—and the handsome attorney who lends a hand.

Arlene James has written over fifty titles for Silhouette Books, and her expertise shows. *So Dear to My Heart* is a tender, original story of a woman finding happiness again. And Karen Rose Smith—another popular veteran—brings us *Doctor in Demand*, about a wounded man who's healed by the love of a woman and her child.

And two newer authors round out the list! Melissa McClone's *His Band of Gold* is an emotional realization of the power of love, and Sue Swift debuts in Silhouette Romance with *His Baby, Her Heart*, in which a woman agrees to fulfill her late sister's dream of children. It's an unusual and powerful story that is part of our THE BABY'S SECRET series.

Enjoy these stories, and make time to appreciate yourselves in your hectic lives! Have a wonderful summer.

Happy reading!

Mary-Theresa Hussey

Mary-Theresa Hussey
Senior Editor

Please address questions and book requests to:
Silhouette Reader Service
U.S.: 3010 Walden Ave., P.O. Box 1325, Buffalo, NY 14269
Canadian: P.O. Box 609, Fort Erie, Ont. L2A 5X3

So Dear to My Heart

ARLENE JAMES

SILHOUETTE *Romance*®

Published by Silhouette Books

America's Publisher of Contemporary Romance

If you purchased this book without a cover you should be aware
that this book is stolen property. It was reported as "unsold and
destroyed" to the publisher, and neither the author nor the
publisher has received any payment for this "stripped book."

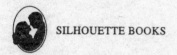

SILHOUETTE BOOKS

ISBN 0-373-19535-4

SO DEAR TO MY HEART

Copyright © 2001 by Deborah Rather

All rights reserved. Except for use in any review, the reproduction
or utilization of this work in whole or in part in any form by any
electronic, mechanical or other means, now known or hereafter
invented, including xerography, photocopying and recording, or in
any information storage or retrieval system, is forbidden without
the written permission of the editorial office, Silhouette Books,
300 East 42nd Street, New York, NY 10017 U.S.A.

All characters in this book have no existence outside the imagination of
the author and have no relation whatsoever to anyone bearing the same
name or names. They are not even distantly inspired by any individual
known or unknown to the author, and all incidents are pure invention.

This edition published by arrangement with Harlequin Books S.A.

® and TM are trademarks of Harlequin Books S.A., used under license.
Trademarks indicated with ® are registered in the United States Patent
and Trademark Office, the Canadian Trade Marks Office and in other
countries.

Visit Silhouette at www.eHarlequin.com

Printed in U.S.A.

Books by Arlene James

ARLENE JAMES

grew up in Oklahoma and has lived all over the South. The author enjoys traveling with her husband, "the most romantic man in the world," but writing has always been her chief pastime.

**Praise for beloved author Arlene James,
in recognition of her**

for Silhouette!

* * *

MR. RIGHT NEXT DOOR
"Be prepared for more realism and depth
than is usually found in a category romance."
—*The Romance Reader*

THE PERFECT WEDDING
"Ms. James provides a powerful inspirational message
for romance fans."
—*Romantic Times Magazine*

DESPERATELY SEEKING DADDY
"Arlene James creates a wonderful heroine
with whom readers will identify…"
—*Romantic Times Magazine*

MARRYING AN OLDER MAN
"I can honestly say that this book fits the gem category."
—*Desert Isle Reviews*

"…Ms. James's complex characters and unhurried pace
make this a rewarding reading experience."
—*Romantic Times Magazine*

Chapter One

Winston slowed the battered pickup truck as soon as he could read the name on the mailbox wired to a fence post at the side of the paved, two-lane road. The engine chugged as he downshifted, causing the old truck to lurch, and he glanced with mild concern across the cab at the dog hanging out the window, its white-tufted black ears flapping in the breeze. Did the animal know that it was going home? He wouldn't have put it past the canny black-and-white dog. Perhaps that was why his son had taken such a liking to it.

For some reason the quiet eight-year-old had formed a deep affection for the odd cattle dog in the months since Dorinda Thacker had left it with them while she went for an extended visit with her sister in Texas. None of the other dogs around the Champlain ranch had ever inspired such devotion from Jamesy, but the dog belonged to the Thacker place, and since Dorinda had returned, so must the mutt. Out here on the sparsely populated Wyoming plains, a good dog was highly valued as useful for working cattle, companionship, keeping wild critters away from the home place, sounding alarms and, in the case of this particular pooch, going for help at a spoken command. Anyone living alone in these parts definitely needed a dog. It was just a shame, for Jamesy's sake, that in Dorinda Thacker's case it had to be this dog.

At least, Winston mused, he could get his stolen cattle back now, not that he had any intention of serving her with the restitution order immediately. After what her ex-husband Bud had put her through—the loss of her savings, the embarrassment of his thieving, the trial and conviction and, of course, the divorce— the woman deserved a chance to get her feet under her before she got hit with the loss of forty head of her cattle. It seemed unfair in a way that she should have to make the restitution, but that was how the court ordered it at the behest of the insurance company. They'd expected her back a couple months ago, in the late spring. It was full summer now, and Dorinda had notified no one, not even the Summerses who were still taking care of her horses, of the reason for her delay. Nevertheless, Win figured that he'd waited this long for his cattle; he could wait awhile yet. The dog was another matter.

With the truck sufficiently slowed, Winston turned it off the paved road onto the narrow dirt track that wound through the small hillocks and shallow rises which provided the Thacker cabin with some shelter from the elements. Win admitted to himself that he felt a little uneasy. Dorinda had often made him uncomfortable. Owing to his personal experience, Win had a little problem with married women who pursued men other than their husbands. It wasn't that he didn't like Dorinda. Not even all that Bud had put her through during their short marriage had dimmed her sunny disposition and happy-go-lucky attitude. Plus, she was a very attractive woman. When it came right down to it, however, he wasn't at all sure that he could ever trust her.

As he guided the truck along the snaky path toward the cabin, he pictured her in his mind. Of medium height, with neat, graceful curves, Dorinda had big brown eyes, a heart-shaped face and a wealth of long, dark hair. She wore a touch too much makeup for his taste and, in his opinion, bought her jeans at least a size too small, but her smile was often so bright that it obscured everything else. He wished, heartily, that she had not made her interest in him so very obvious before Bud had been arrested. Perhaps all that had happened and the months away had changed her. He hoped so. Six years was a long time for a man to be alone, and lately he'd been feeling it more acutely than ever before, which was why he'd been out driving alone late last night and had spotted the light in Dorinda's window. He'd tried to call this morning, but the phone had not been reconnected, so he'd decided to drive over instead.

The small, weather-grayed house came into view. Perched as it was halfway up the gentle rise of the shallow hill behind it, the cabin boasted very little front yard, and Dorinda's flashy red truck took up what was there, so Win circled around and parked at the end of the narrow porch. After he killed the engine, he reached across to ruffle the ears of the black-and-white collie, which looked at him with inscrutable black eyes rimmed with a narrow, caramel brown mask resembling a pair of lopsided spectacles.

"You're home, old son. We'll miss you back at The Champ, but Dorinda needs you here. You take care of her now."

The dog yawned widely, as if to say that he knew his business well and needed no reminders from some scruffy cowboy. Winston chuckled and reached into his shirt pocket for a short, splintered stick, which the dog nipped carefully from his fingertips, white-feathered black tail wagging happily. Win let himself out of the truck and waited for the dog to leap down to the ground before walking around his truck and between Dorinda's and the porch to the narrow, sagging center steps, the dog at his heels.

As Winston drew close he could see through the screen and the open door to the kitchen beyond. Empty. The dog dropped down onto its belly on the porch and began gnawing the stick, which it held upright between its front paws. Rapping his knuckles on the door frame, Win called out, "Hello! Winston Champlain here."

For a moment, he heard nothing in response. Then tentative footsteps came from the direction of the living area. Immediately, the dog began to growl, much to Winston's confusion. A shadowy form appeared, accompanied by a soft, rusty female voice.

"What do you want?"

At that, the dog shot up to its feet and began barking. Perplexed and surprised by the animal's reaction,

Win commanded sharply, "Down!" The animal obeyed, but reluctantly, dropping onto its haunches and quieting to a whine. Win pulled the screen door open so they could see one another better, propping one shoulder against it. "Hey, there."

Further comment evaporated as he stared at the woman standing before him. She was thinner than before, her long T-shirt bagging unexpectedly around her slender frame and revealing long, delectable legs. An utter lack of cosmetics revealed a pretty face more delicate and vulnerable than he remembered, but the most surprising element of her appearance was the short hair. The long, heavy fall of brown-black had been transformed into a wispy cap that seemed to enlarge her warm brown eyes and call attention to the plumpness of her dusky pink mouth and the graceful length of her neck.

Win realized that his mouth was hanging open only when he used it to exclaim, "Wow!" Her brows beetled at that, and she folded her arms. Win shook away his speechlessness and found a compliment. "I—I mean, I really like your hair, Dorinda."

A soft gasp was his only warning before she stepped back, reached out and slammed the door, literally, in his face.

A full minute passed before he could grasp the reality of what had happened. Even then, it made no sense. Unless she meant to fight the restitution order. Suddenly, his blood boiled.

He'd been darn patient about this. Everyone from whom Bud had stolen got their cattle back but him, and he'd be skinned for a polecat before he swallowed the loss of forty producing heifers. He felt bad for her, but the law said that Dorinda, who had received the ranch and the Thacker herd in her divorce settlement, was responsible for reimbursing him. Bud couldn't very well come up with either cattle or their cash equivalent from a prison cell, and he had testified that the proceeds of his thieving had been put back into the place he'd inherited from his uncle, so that left Dorinda on the hook.

Winston turned on his heel and stomped across the porch and down the steps. The dog followed, and Win was of no mind to discourage it. He yanked open the cab door of the truck and waited for the dog to climb up inside. Muttering under his breath about capricious women, he got in and started the engine. The dog whined as Win backed the truck away from the house. The sound had a quality about it with which Win could readily identify.

"I know what you mean, boy, but she hasn't heard the last of us, not by a long shot."

Danica lifted her head from the kitchen table. A dull ache bulged deep within her ears, and her eyes were swollen, a condition with which she was too often plagued since the death of her beloved sister. Even now, some two months after the fact, she couldn't quite believe that Dorinda was gone. The entire past year and a half had been one catastrophe after another.

First Dori had met Bud and, despite Danica's misgivings, married him after a whirlwind courtship. Then the newlyweds had moved to Wyoming, leaving Danica to struggle alone with the full rent of an apartment that had been meant for two. As if to add insult

to injury, the pediatrician for whom Danica worked
as a nurse had taken for a partner none other than
Danica's philandering ex-husband, Michael. Over the
following months, Michael had attempted to reignite
their relationship, Bud had been caught rustling cattle
and was sentenced to prison, Dori had gotten a divorce and returned home to Texas to decide what to
do next. And finally had come the awful accident that
had cost Dorinda her life.

Danica told herself that a lesser woman would have
buckled under all the strain, but she knew that she
was holding on by her fingernails. Her reaction to
Winston Champlain's unexpected appearance today
was proof of that. And yet, the reaction was somewhat
justifiable, wasn't it?

For weeks and weeks after returning home, Dori
had alternately complained about her ex-husband and
rhapsodized about their nearest neighbor, Winston
Champlain. She'd waffled between returning to the
entertainments and sophistication of Dallas for good
and the supposed joys of actually owning her own
ranch in Wyoming, however remote. Even after her
normally ebullient spirits and natural penchant for fun
had reasserted themselves, she had troubled Danica
by measuring every man she met by the growing en-
ticements of Champlain. Finally she had confessed to
a "special relationship" with the man. Thoroughly
alarmed, Dani had begged Dori to sell the ranch and
stay with her in Dallas.

At length, Dorinda had agreed. Danica had ar-
ranged to take a few days off to accompany her sister
back to Wyoming to settle her business affairs and
put the ranch on the market. They were in the vicinity

of Tucumcari, New Mexico, driving Danica's small coupe in order to save on gasoline, when Dorinda had cut in front of a tractor-trailer rig only to find the traffic in front of them braking to avoid a garbage bag tumbling across the six-lane highway in a stiff breeze. The resulting crash had given Danica nightmares for weeks. The worst of it, however, had been waking up in the hospital with a smashing headache but hardly a scratch otherwise to find that the person dearest to her in all the world was no longer a part of it.

The weeks following had been unbearable. Danica had emerged from the initial fog of grief in a confused state of mind. She'd found it difficult to concentrate on work or much of anything, really. The well-meaning condolences and advice of friends and co-workers had been especially difficult to take, and Dani had found herself reacting with surprising anger. Just two weeks after returning to her job, she'd taken a leave of absence and retreated to the relative privacy of her apartment, only to find that her self-appointed caretakers were even more determined to pull her back into everyday life than she'd realized.

Finally, in sheer desperation, she'd packed a suitcase and headed for Wyoming in Dori's gas-guzzling truck, ostensibly to settle whatever unfinished business remained and put the place on the market. She'd taken some ridiculous chances, she realized now, by driving straight through, and the week or more that she'd been here, she'd done little but sleep and stare out across the treeless plains, never seeing another soul until Winston Champlain, of all people, had arrived at her door.

The irony of it was not lost on Danica. Here she

was right where she'd begged her sister not to go, and the first person she sees is the very one she least wants to. Now that she was over the shock of it, she was rather surprised to find that Dorinda had not exaggerated his physical appeal. Standing at least three inches over six feet, he had that kind of lean, rangy strength about him that many athletes possessed. His hair—though mostly hidden by a dusty gray felt hat with a wide, curly brim and high, domed crown—was a light, biscuit brown and fanned out in undisciplined flips from the nape of his neck. Slightly darker brows slashed straight across his face in two short dashes above light, smoke-gray eyes of startling clarity. It was a strong face, strong enough to carry a square, slightly cleft chin, prominent cheekbones and a long, slender nose that had obviously been broken at least once above a wide, spare mouth.

No wonder Dori had allowed herself to become entangled with him. How easy it must have been for him to slip beneath her defenses after the deep disappointment of her marriage to Bud, and now, clearly, he was ready to resume the affair. Obviously, she should have told him about Dorinda, but she'd been so shocked to see him standing there just as Dori had described him that she'd been tongue-tied. Then to hear her sister's name on his lips, with a compliment, no less, had been more than Danica could bear. She'd slammed the door in his face and dissolved in tears.

How long ago that might have been, she didn't really know, but a hollowness in her middle reminded her that she hadn't eaten all day. She put her head in her hands and contemplated the necessity of it, dredging up the will to rise from her chair and go to the pantry. Fortunately, since the refrigerator didn't work, the larder was well-stocked with nonperishable food-stuffs. Unfortunately, with neither microwave nor functioning cookstove, she was reduced to eating her irregular meals cold right out of the can, box or bag. At least she had electricity and, therefore, hot water, though why that had not been shut off she had no idea.

Forcing herself to her feet, she went to the pantry and selected a can at random, carried it to the counter and opened it. Corn. She hated canned corn. Fresh or even frozen was much better, in her opinion. With a sigh she picked up the spoon left on the counter after her last meal and carried it to the table along with the can. She got down three bites before a pounding at her door made her start so violently that she turned over the can, spilling the contents across the table top.

"I want to talk to you!"

Him! An uncontrollable anger seized her. How dare he intrude like this again! She balled up both fists and shouted at the door, "Go away!"

"Fat chance, lady! You can't just brush this off!"

"Go away!" she cried again, but somewhat feebly, her energy quickly waning. She looked at the spilled corn and felt close to tears once more. Just then the door, which she had neglected to lock, opened and Winston Champlain strode through it, waving a folded, blue-backed paper.

"Look," he said sharply, "I wanted to do this easy after all you've been through, but by golly, one way or another, I mean to have my cattle!" He shook the paper out and thrust it in her face, adding, "You're served! Now what the hell are you gonna do about it?''

Served? Danica stared openmouthed at the paper held to the end of her nose, but her eyes crossed when she tried to bring the words into focus. Irritably, she pushed it away.

''You're not welcome here, Champlain, so go away.''

''Well, that's just fine!'' he snapped. ''First Bud and now you. I guess you're as much thief as him.''

''I am not!''

''Yeah, well, what do you call it? I'm out forty producing heifers, and the court says you're the one who has to reimburse me for them!''

Forty heifers? Holy cow, her dad had never owned so many at one time. Of course, cattle had just been a sideline with him. His cotton crop had been his main concern back then. ''Where on earth would I get forty heifers?'' she demanded.

''Out of your herd, presumably.''

''My herd?'' Oh. Of course. She hadn't thought of that. As her sister's only surviving relative, the ranch and the cattle would be hers now. ''I don't even know if I have forty heifers.''

''Guess we'll find out, won't we?'' With a sharp flick of his wrist, he swirled the paper at her. She caught it in midair, crumpling one side in her fist, and turned it right side up. It was, indeed, a restitution order from the circuit court. ''Read it and weep, Dorinda,'' he said snidely.

She sighed and lifted her wrist to her forehead. ''I'm not Dorinda.''

He literally snorted. "Huh! You don't expect me to believe that."

She stared at him, suddenly fatigued again, tears filling her eyes as she searched for the words. "Dorinda is... There was a-an a-accident." She carried the paper to the counter and carefully laid it there, one hand going to her hip, the other to her chest. "I—I didn't know about this. I would've t-told someone if I had."

"Told someone?" he echoed uncertainly.

"About Dori," she whispered, holding onto the ragged tail of her composure by a mere thread. "It was only t-two months ago. In Tucumcari. O-on our way h-here."

"An accident," he said stupidly.

She pulled a deep breath, blinked and nodded. "I'm her sister, Danica. Danica Lynch."

He tilted his head, staring at her, and finally concluded, "Her *twin* sister."

"Yes."

"And Dorinda was in an accident."

"That's right."

Concern and regret creased his features. Reaching up, he removed his hat, as if just then remembering his manners. He cleared his throat. "How is she? Where is she?"

Dani tried to tell him and couldn't. The effort sent fresh tears rolling down her face. Finally, he understood what she couldn't say; she saw it in his eyes the instant before he blurted, "Oh, my God, she's dead!"

That awful, final word again. Dead. It pierced her through with such force that it doubled her over. The next thing she knew, she was cradled against a solid chest, long, strong arms wrapped around her.

"Merciful heaven, I'm so sorry. I had no idea. Oh, man, I came busting in here like a crazy man, accusing you of trying to cheat me when you didn't even know what I was talking about! And all the time your sister..." He tightened his embrace and dropped his voice. "I am so sorry. Poor Dorinda!"

Being held like this felt as comfortable as a warm blanket on a cold day. Danica closed her eyes, imbued with a sense of safety and indulgence. For the first time she considered that, eventually, it might be okay, after all.

"I should've told you earlier," she admitted, breathing through her mouth as tears clogged her nose. "I was just so shocked when you called me by her name."

"I'm sorry about that," he apologized sincerely, "but you've got to admit that you look an awful lot alike."

She managed a doleful nod. "We're identical, except for the hair, but you obviously had no way of knowing that."

His big hand stroked the back of her head, and he whispered, "I do like your hair. Very much. That was no mistake, at least."

A thrill of pleasure shot through her. She lifted her head to thank him for the compliment, looked up into his rugged face, saw the flare of awareness that warmed his cool gray eyes—and abruptly realized what she was doing and with whom! Jerking back, she broke the embrace. "I, uh, that is..."

His brow beetled with obvious concern, and he reached out a hand to her. "Are you all right?"

"Oh, uh, I'm not feeling very well."

"Maybe you ought to—"

"It's just a headache," she interrupted. "It'll be fine."

Nodding, he glanced around the room. His gaze settled, and he frowned. She followed his line of sight and lifted one hand to hide her smile. His hat lay right in the middle of her spilled corn. Obviously he had discarded it rather hastily earlier. Remembering why, she cleared her throat and glanced away as he gingerly retrieved the hat and brushed at the stains.

"Listen, I oughta be going," he said. "We'll work out the restitution thing later. Is there anything I can do for you before I go?"

"Uh, no, thank you. I don't need a thing," she refused firmly, wanting only to get rid of him now.

"If you do, don't hesitate to ask," he told her. "My folks were fond of Dorinda. They're going to be real shocked and saddened by this. I know they'll want to do something, especially Mom." He glanced around again, adding, "Maybe you'd like her to come over and help you straighten the place up?"

Danica looked around her, realizing for the first time that she'd let things get out of hand since she'd been here. Garbage spilled out of a full container. The mess on the table was spreading. Utensils and tin can lids littered the kitchen counter. Articles of discarded clothing lay strewn about the tiny living area, including, to her extreme embarrassment, one of her bras!

Coloring violently, she put her hand to her head, hoping to anchor his attention there, and said weakly,

"That's very kind, but I'll take care of it as soon as I get rid of this headache."

"Do you have something to take for that?" he asked, voice heavy with concern.

"Of course, I do. I'm a nurse, after all."

"Are you? That's good."

"The thing is," she lied, "it's going to make me sleepy, so if you don't mind..."

"Oh. Right." He put on the hat and turned for the door, saying, "I'll check in on you tomorrow."

"No, don't bother," she said quickly. "I'm fine, really."

"No bother," he assured her, smiling warmly as he opened the door and slipped through it. "That's what neighbors are for."

Neighbors. Danica closed her eyes and bowed her head as the door closed behind him. Something told her that as a neighbor Winston Champlain was going to be as much a problem for her as for her sister. But in another way, of course. She certainly was in no danger of becoming enamored of the man. She knew his kind far too well for that.

Dismayed by the lack of reassurance brought by that thought, Danica turned her attention back to the small, L-shaped, living and kitchen area. Why hadn't she realized how cluttered the place had become? The answer to that was obvious. Disgusted with herself, she straightened her spine and dashed away the last of her tears with the back of one hand.

"All right, Danica," she told herself aloud. "Time to get a grip. You need order and exercise. No more lying around the house twenty-four hours a day. No more being a slob. No more maudlin self-indulgence.'' And no more being charmed by the likes of Winston Champlain, she added silently.

She'd learned her lesson with charming men the hard way, and if that wasn't enough, she had Dorinda's experience to consider, as well. True, unlike Bud Thacker, Michael had never stolen so much as a tongue depressor, so far as Danica knew, and he was a fine physician. That didn't change the fact that he had professed love to the devoted little wife at home, namely her, then carried on with half the nurses in Dallas as easily as he dispensed pills and treats to the children who came through his examining room, while remaining one of the more likable men she'd ever known.

Winston Champlain was every bit as attractive, charming and likable as Michael—when he wasn't shouting. If he somehow seemed...stronger, as well, that hardly signified. The man had been involved with her sister. He'd taken advantage of Dorinda's abysmal experience in her marriage and used her own vulnerability against her.

Danica frowned. Funny, he hadn't behaved quite like a man who had just lost the woman with whom he was romantically involved. No doubt it had been very casual as far as he was concerned. Obviously Dorinda had been much more emotionally involved. Wasn't the woman *always* more engaged emotionally? Well, not her. She didn't, couldn't, wouldn't care a fig for the likes of Winston Champlain—no matter how good-looking he was or how wonderful he smelled, a unique combination of leather, smoke, mint and something she couldn't quite define. No, it didn't matter how safe she'd felt snuggled there against his chest, she knew what she knew, and that was the end of it.

Snatching up a dish towel, she went to the sink and moistened it before beginning to scoop the corn back into the can.

Chapter Two

"It's okay, boy," Jamesy told the dog, patting the sleek black head between the ears. "I'll come see you real soon, I promise."

Win sighed mentally. He'd had no luck getting off without the boy this morning, but once he'd explained that Dorinda's sister had taken up residence at the Thacker place, Jamesy had known that the dog must go home. When he had bravely offered to tell "Miss Lynch" what the old dog "liked best to keep happy," Winston had known that he couldn't leave the child behind. It would have been easier to do this alone, but he felt that he had to honor his son's generosity and courage by taking him along. After all, since Jamesy could walk and talk, Win had tried to teach the boy the importance of doing the right thing. Now he had to let him actually go through with it. He only hoped that Danica appreciated the boy's effort.

They rounded the final bend in the narrow dirt road

and pulled up in the same spot where Win had previously parked. Jamesy looked up, tilting his head far back in order to see past the wide, curled brim of his stained hat. Once off-white but now a mottled gray/tan, the hat was and always had been too big for the boy. The tall, round, felt crown had been spotted by an unexpected rain a few years earlier. Such heavy rainfall was so much a rarity in these dry plains that Jamesy had since worn the stains as a kind of badge of honor. Blowing dust, honest perspiration, falling snow and the occasional beverage gone awry had done the rest, but Jamesy had rejected all replacements. Win always thought the stained, too-big hat gave the boy a pathetic air. His sadness over the dog only added to it.

"Don't worry, son. Everything will be fine."

"It's okay, Dad," Jamesy promised, determination not quite covering the waver in his voice. "Twig and me've talked it over, and way we see it, nothing much is changing. We can still be special friends even if we ain't at the same place no more."

"Aren't," Winston corrected automatically. Then he smiled and clamped a hand onto the boy's thin shoulder, saying, "Have I told you lately how proud I am of you?"

Jamesy just gave him a watery smile and shook his head, glancing down at the dog again. Knowing that he could say nothing to make it better, Win opened the door and got out. Jamesy followed his lead, getting out on the other side of the truck. The dog dropped down onto the ground beside him, and together they waited until Win came around and joined them. They walked single file alongside Dorinda's, rather, Danica's truck and up onto the porch, where Winston wagged a finger at the dog.

"No more of that barking, now."

With that Jamesy dropped down onto his haunches and wrapped both arms around the dog, obviously intending to quell any outburst. Winston knocked and waited for the door to open. When she didn't immediately answer, he wondered if they'd come too early. It was going on half past eight, but Danica might be a late sleeper. He'd have called and set up a convenient time if the phone was working. As it was, he just had to take his chances. Finally, the inner door swung back.

"Oh," she said through the screen. "I guess you want to talk about the restitution order. I did read it last night."

"Actually, I, that is, my boy Jamesy and I brought your dog back."

"Dog?" she echoed, frowning. "What dog?"

"This dog," Winston explained, pointing downward. Finally she opened the screen and stepped out onto the porch. She was wearing sweats and socks, and from the way she went to smoothing her frazzled hair, he suspected that she'd slept in them.

"I don't know this dog," she said.

"This here's Twig," Jamesy told her, ruffling the dog's black-and-white fur. "He's a real good 'un." As he spoke, the dog laved his face with its pale pink tongue.

"Okay," Danica said uncertainly, "but he's not my dog."

"He belongs to the place," Winston explained. "Old Ned, Bud's uncle, used to train the best working dogs in this whole area. He raised Twig from a pup and trained him special. When your sister left here, she asked us to take care of him.''

''Well, then take care of him,'' Danica said, watching the dog flop over so Jamesy could vigorously rub his belly. ''It has nothing to do with me.''

''But he belongs to the place,'' Winston pointed out again. ''That means he's yours.''

''I don't want him,'' she retorted. ''You keep him.''

''Oh, boy!'' Jamesy exclaimed. ''Did you hear that, Twig?''

Winston frowned, wondering how this had gotten so complicated. ''Listen,'' he said to her, ''you don't understand. The dog belongs to you.''

''But I don't want him, and the boy obviously does,'' she pointed out.

''Can I keep him then, Dad?''

Winston sighed, exasperated. ''No, you can't keep him, son. Miss Lynch doesn't know what she's saying.''

''The hell I don't! Why would I want to be bothered with some mutt?''

''I told you,'' Winston said through his teeth, patience wearing awfully thin. ''He's a highly trained, valuable, working dog, and he comes with the place to you.''

She folded her arms. ''Well, I'm not keeping him, so just take him back where you brought him from.''

Win threw up his hands. ''I can't do that. You don't even have the telephone working yet.''

''And I don't intend to,'' she told him smartly. ''What has that got to do with anything?''

"For Pete's sake, woman, will you just listen to reason for a minute?" he erupted hotly.

"Oh, so now I'm unreasonable, am I?" She parked her hands on her hips and glared at him. "Well, if that's the way you're going to behave, I'll thank you to take your stupid dog and get off my land."

"He's not my dog!" Winston roared.

"And he's not stupid," Jamesy added defensively. Winston looked down, ashamed and embarrassed that he'd shouted at a grieving woman in front of his son. Even the dog was staring at the two of them, its head tilted to one side.

Danica had the grace to look chagrined. "I'm sure he's not," she told Jamesy in a kinder, if stern tone, "but I don't want to take care of a dog."

"He don't take much caring for, miss," Jamesy told her.

"I don't even know how long I'll be here," Danica protested impatiently. "He'll be better off with you."

"But you need a dog," Winston reasoned.

Her pointed little chin came up at an obstinate angle. "Don't try to tell me what I need! How would you know what I need?"

His temper slipped free. "Lady, you absolutely take the cake! You won't listen to plain sense!"

She threw a finger at his pickup truck. "Get off my land!"

"Of all the hardheaded, idiotic women!"

"Take your kid and his dog and go!" she shouted. Jamesy lurched to his feet then, catching Danica's attention. "What are you waiting for?" she demanded of the boy. "Get out of here!"

Jamesy took off at a run, stomping down the porch

steps in his heavy boots. Twig whined, looked at Danica, then went after the boy. Winston was mad enough to spit nails into an iron bar, but before he could say anything else to her, she stepped inside and slammed the door again. He considered pushing his way in and making her see reason, but Jamesy's presence restrained him.

Reluctantly, he turned away and followed Jamesy to the truck, his concern for her reckless behavior beginning to push away his anger. Someone needed to have a stern talk with that woman, and he reckoned it would have to be him. He didn't much like the notion, but she had to see how foolish it would be for her stay out here all on her own without a dog. Didn't she realize that it was a thirty-five-minute drive to his place, and that he and his family were her closest neighbors? What if something happened to her? Maybe the dog would do her no good, but at least the chance existed if the dog was around.

Win settled behind the steering wheel and looked over at his son. Twig was sitting in Jamesy's lap, its nose stuck to the window. This was getting to be a habit, dragging that old collie over here and then dragging it back again. Winston lifted off his hat and plowed a hand through his thick, wavy hair.

"What's wrong with her, Dad?" Jamesy asked suddenly. "Is it because of me? Don't she like kids?"

Winston sighed. He hadn't wanted to explain the full situation to his son, but that seemed the best thing now. It was bad enough when a boy's mother walked away without a backward glance; it was beyond standing for when a rude neighbor made him feel disliked and responsible for problems with which he had nothing to do.

"It's not you, son, not at all. Miss Lynch, she's going through some hard times now. You saw how much she looks like Mrs. Thacker who used to own this place?"

"A whole bunch," Jamesy agreed.

"That's because Mrs. Thacker and Miss Lynch are twins. Or they were. That's the problem, son. I don't like to tell you this, but Miss Lynch's sister was in an accident a couple months ago, and Miss Lynch is still feeling the loss real bad."

The boy's eyes had grown large as Winston spoke. "You mean that Mrs. Thacker got killed?"

"I'm afraid so."

Jamesy pushed his hat back as he pondered that awful truth. "Man," he said, "that stinks."

Winston's eyebrows rose slightly at the phrasing. "You're absolutely right."

Jamesy patted the dog's rump absently. "Maybe Miss Lynch just don't want to get to like old Twig, you know, in case he goes off or the coyotes get him or something."

Winston stared at his son's small earnest face, a certain pride swelling in him. "You may be right about that, too, son."

Jamesy sighed and, with the pragmatism of a child for whom things had pretty much worked out as he'd hoped, said, "If she don't want him, though, I guess there's nothing anybody can do, huh?"

"I guess not," Winston murmured, reaching for the keys he'd left hanging in the ignition. He wouldn't have bet, however, that the matter was resolved, and when he woke the next morning to see his son's worried face hovering over him, he knew it for a fact.

"Well, at least you're not a picky eater," Danica said to the dog slurping down a can of beef and vegetable soup from a bowl on the kitchen floor. The mutt had shown up in the middle of the night, whining and scratching at her door, a stick of some sort in its mouth. She'd tried to send it home, but when she'd opened the screen to shoo it off her porch, it had dashed inside and made a beeline for the rug in front of the old gas stove tucked into the corner of the living room, where it promptly began chewing up the stick. She'd let it stay the night since it had been too late to try to take it back to the boy where it belonged, but she still intended to do that, even if she had found an odd comfort in the animal's silent companionship.

With no television, Danica had begun to find the evenings rather long of late. The day before she had discovered a stack of country and western music tapes in a box behind the sofa. That had sent her on a search for something with which to play them and led her to a cache of paperback novels and magazines beneath the bed and an old boom box in the bedroom closet. Danica was delighted, and the evening that followed was the most pleasant she'd experienced in some time. Nevertheless, listening to music and reading had proven more satisfying somehow with that mutt lying there on the rug.

Still, no matter how determined the Champlains might be to argue, she wouldn't be responsible for parting a child from his pet. Their behavior frankly puzzled her. She couldn't imagine a father who wouldn't be delighted with that determination on her part, but then she had never imagined a man like Winston Champlain.

The dog licked the plate clean and sat back on its haunches, as if to ask, "Now what?"

"Now we get you home," Danica said aloud, rising to her feet and slinging the strap of her hand bag over one shoulder. "Come on."

She wasn't exactly certain in which direction the Champlain ranch lay, but given that the road only ran in two directions with no intersections for miles and miles, it couldn't be too difficult to find. It wasn't as if she didn't have plenty of time to look. They didn't make it off the porch before Winston Champlain's old truck slewed into view, however. Danica leaned a shoulder against the support post of the porch roof and waited, arms folded, while he parked, got out and walked around to the bottom of the steps.

"I figured the dog had come here," he said.

Danica looked down at the dog sitting beside her, determined to remain aloof and unaffected, despite the sudden leap of her pulse. "He showed up late last night."

"When we found him gone this morning, I told everyone that Twig had just gone home, but Jamesy was worried, so I figured I'd better check it out." He leaned down and patted the dog's head, saying, "You know what you're doing, don't you, Twig?"

"Appropriate name," Danica commented. "He had a stick in his mouth when he showed up last night."

"Yeah, nothing he likes better than a piece of wood

to chew on,'' Winston told her, straightening. "I figure his insides are full of splinters by now. It's sort of a mystery where he gets them, but he always seems to have one about four inches long around somewhere.''

Suddenly the dog went up onto all fours and bristled, growling low in its throat. "What is it, boy?" Winston asked.

Danica followed its line of sight to the horizon, shading her eyes with one hand. "Is that a coyote?"

"Looks like it. They're pretty bold when there's no known opposition.'' The dog barked, and the coyote loped away over the rise. Winston pushed back his hat and braced one foot on the bottom step. "That's one reason a dog like Twig is handy to have around.''

"So I see. All the more reason you should keep him. I was just bringing him back to you, by the way.''

Winston shook his head. "Let me tell you about this dog,'' he said, parking his hands at his hips. "He's probably the best working cow dog in the business, but that's just part of it. He's trained for any number of things, protection, guarding, barking an alarm. He'll even go for help if you tell him to. Once, on a cold winter day Ned's horse fell with him, broke its leg, and Ned couldn't get free. Ned sent Twig for help. Saved his life, no doubt about it. Another time, Ned, who was getting on up in years, slipped getting out of the tub and knocked himself unconscious. Don't guess we'll ever know how Twig got out of the house. Ned was up and nursing a goose egg by the time we got here, but it could've gone the other way. When Ned passed—went real peaceful in his sleep—Twig came, then, too.''

"Wow," Danica said, looking down at the dog with new respect. "You're a regular Lassie, aren't you, fella? And I guess the boy is your Timmy."

"Actually," Winston said, "that would be you. The dog belongs here."

She looked him in the eye and said flatly, "It belongs with the boy."

Cool gray eyes assessed then pulled back from hers. "Looks to me like Twig has something to say about that. Voted with his feet, apparently, and it seems you're elected."

She frowned. "But I saw how fond your son is of him."

"His name's Jamesy."

"Jamesy," she repeated impatiently, "fine. You tell Jamesy that Twig belongs with him now."

Winston Champlain shook his head again, wagging it decisively from side to side. "I'd say Twig has other ideas."

She looked down at the dog, sighed and bit her lip. "I couldn't live with myself, knowing how the, er, Jamesy would miss him."

"Is that why you threw us off the place yesterday?" he asked softly.

She couldn't quite bring herself to meet his gaze. "You wouldn't listen to me."

"Now if that isn't the pot calling the kettle black."

He had a way of being right, blast him. "I just didn't want to fight about it, okay?"

"You didn't have to be rude."

"I wasn't—" She broke off, knowing that he was right *again* and confessed, "You made me mad."

"Yeah, well, that was no reason to talk to the boy the way you did."

Her surprised gaze popped up to his face before she could prevent it. "I wasn't angry with him! Anything, ah, heated that I might have said was aimed at you."

"I know that," he admitted, "but Jamesy's kind of sensitive."

"Really," she quipped drolly, "and he's your son?"

His mouth thinned into a flat line. "That wasn't funny."

Her eyebrows jumped. Apparently she'd hit a tender spot for which she hadn't really aimed. "Sorry."

"The fact is," Winston Champlain told her angrily, ignoring her muttered apology, "he looks exactly like me, in case you didn't notice."

"I noticed," she said softly, but he wasn't satisfied with that.

"Jamesy couldn't be anyone else's," Winston insisted, "no matter how his mother behaved after he was born."

Danica winced. Oh, boy, had she put her foot in it. "I only meant to imply that you aren't very sensitive yourself," she told him sheepishly. It wasn't at all true, she admitted silently, his current reaction a case in point.

"It's bad enough that she abandoned us for the party life," he went on heatedly, "without you making him think you don't like him, too."

She blanched, truly ashamed now. "Oh, gosh, he didn't really think that, did he?"

"That's exactly what he thought! He's a kid, and a kid whose own mom didn't think enough of him to stick around."

She moaned, eyes squeezed shut. "Me and my big mouth! I don't know what's wrong with me anymore. I have no patience. My fuse is so short! I just didn't want to take the boy's dog, and you wouldn't accept that, so I lost it. I certainly never meant to make him think that I didn't like him."

Winston folded his arms and heaped on the coals. "You did more than that, frankly. You didn't appreciate the sacrifice he was making in order to do the right thing. Yes, he's fond of the dog, but he realizes that it belongs here. What's more, Jamesy's got sense enough to know that you need that dog, even if you don't."

She had her own opinion about that, but she wasn't going to argue about it now. It didn't matter at this point that she wasn't going to get caught under a fallen horse or slip getting out of the bathtub. As unfair as it seemed, she'd survived a horrendous car crash; she couldn't believe anything worse could happen to her. That, however, was not the issue.

"What can I do?" she asked simply, and he told her.

"Just let me tell Jamesy that he can come visit Twig occasionally."

"That's it?"

"You were maybe thinking of adopting him?"

She rolled her eyes, but the truth was that she wouldn't be leaving herself open to much more interaction with Winston Champlain if she did adopt his son. He wasn't really giving her any options, however, and she couldn't seem to find any for herself.

Sighing inwardly, she nodded and said, "Tell Jamesy for me that he's welcome any time, that I wasn't shouting at *him* yesterday, and that I'm looking forward to getting to know him. And tell him that I'll take good care of Twig."

Winston Champlain shoved his hat farther back on his head and sent her a lazy, approving smile with just enough smugness in it to make her want to hit him. Problem was, he had a right to that smile.

"If it helps, I figure you have good reason to be mad at the world right now," he said.

She grimaced and held up both hands defensively. "We aren't going to grief counseling now, are we, because I've got to warn you, I am not up for it."

He looked down, rubbing his chin. "No fear there, but we could talk about that restitution order."

She looked away, pondering what to say. The truth was that she'd had about all of Winston Champlain that she could take for the moment. He had the most infuriating way of being right about too much, and in her current state of mind, one slip of the tongue, his, and she would be shouting. She'd prefer to avoid that embarrassment.

"Uh, this isn't the best time, actually," she said, hoping he wouldn't press for an explanation. "Why don't we make an appointment for, oh, day after tomorrow?"

He rubbed his chin. "It would have to be that evening."

Relieved, she agreed immediately. "Sure. Evening's fine."

"Say about seven?"

"Seven's good."

His smile beamed pure pleasure this time. "Okay," he said, resettling his hat. "See you then." He leaned forward and ruffled the dog's ear, saying, "You take care of her now, Twig."

The dog snuffled, then yelped in delight when Winston took a short stick from his shirt pocket. Danica marveled at how cleanly the dog nipped it from the cowboy's long, lean fingers. It immediately dropped down onto its belly then and began gnawing.

Winston chuckled, flipped her a wave and walked back to his truck. A few moments later, he and the truck disappeared around the same curve from which they had appeared.

Danica sat down on the step next to the dog. "Well, I tried, but I guess we're a team, after all," she told it, "for now." The dog glanced up at her, then went back to gnawing the stick. "I'd better see what I can scare up to feed you until I can find a store and buy some doggy chow."

She frowned at that, remembering nothing that even resembled a store on the long drive out from Rawlins. Surely she wouldn't have to go all the way back there just to shop. She should've asked Winston. If she didn't find something before she saw him next, she'd make a point of asking during their next meeting. Meanwhile, she'd given herself a little breathing space. Winston Champlain made her feel crowded, threatened, even, though not in any way that she could easily identify.

Well, it didn't matter. After their next meeting, she wouldn't have to really even talk to him again. The boy could visit, just as she'd said, and that undoubtedly meant Winston would have to come along. But their business would be settled by then, and she'd make sure that she was too busy to converse with him. Then, in a few weeks, she'd be out of here. Though she hadn't really thought it through, yet, she'd never meant to stay. Once all the business was taken care of and the ranch was sold, she'd be on her way. To where?

Dallas no longer seemed to hold any appeal, though she supposed that what remained of her life was there. Still, now that she thought of it, she could go anywhere she pleased. If she wasn't quite sure where she was pleased to go, well, she'd figure it out later.

For now, insuring that she could feed this old dog was occupation enough.

Chapter Three

Winston stared into the bathroom mirror as he smoothed his hair back from his forehead with a pair of matching brushes which fit neatly into his palms. While intently studying his image, he realized with dismay that his hair needed a trim. Why hadn't he had his mother get out the scissors and whack off the bottom of it? Impulsively deciding that he should strip off his neatly pressed gray shirt and let her have a go at it right now, he lifted his hand to begin opening the buttons on the heavy cotton placket, which brought his wristwatch into view. One glance showed him that he didn't have time for such indulgences. Sighing richly, he resigned himself to needing a trim and quickly examined his jaw to be sure he hadn't missed a spot during his shave, then hurried from the small room.

Snagging his tan felt dress hat from the top of the dresser in his bedroom, he clumped down the stairs in his freshly polished boots and swung around the newel post to stride down the hall and into his mother's kitchen, the very heart of the house. Suddenly thirsty, he stopped by the sink, ran a glass of cold tap water and drank it down without stopping.

"I'm off," he said to the room in general, turning toward the coatrack beside the door. His gaze caught on the bloodred bloom of one of his mother's summer roses standing in a water-filled jar on the windowsill. Even as he reached for his good jean jacket and slung it on, he pictured himself delivering a big bouquet of the rare beauties to Danica Lynch. She would be surprised, then pleased, and she would look at him in a whole new way, appreciation glimmering in her eyes.

"Earth to Winston," said an amused familiar voice.

Win shook himself free of the ridiculous notion. "Did you say something, Mom?"

As a small, plump woman with dark, graying hair that waved about her face and chin, Madge Champlain was the perfect antithesis to her tall, rawboned, white-haired husband, Buck, who was even now slurping his coffee from a saucer at the table in the center of the room.

"She said, you're looking fine," Buck answered Winston. "What she means is you're mighty well armed for a business discussion."

Madge whacked Buck reprovingly on the shoulder with a dish towel, her blue eyes twinkling. Win cleared his throat self-consciously. What had he been thinking when he put on these snug, well-starched jeans, best shirt, dress hat and freshly polished boots?

This wasn't a date, after all. "Never hurts to make a good impression," he muttered.

"Of course, it doesn't," Madge agreed placatingly.

Buck slurped and added, "'Specially if she's as pretty as her sister."

"More," Jamesy said matter-of-factly, opening a cabinet to take down a box of cookies. Winston and everyone else stared at him in surprise. After a moment, Jamesy realized it and looked around. "Well, she is," he said defensively. "She don't wear all that goop on her face like Mrs. Thacker did, an' I like her hair."

"Doesn't," Winston corrected automatically, thinking that his son and he were more alike than anyone even knew.

"Huh?"

"She *doesn't* wear too much makeup." Madge said to Jamesy. "I think that's what you were trying to say."

"Yeah, okay," the boy mumbled around the cookie he'd bitten into.

Winston went back to the sink for another drink of water. He was feeling unaccountably dry this evening. Better yet, maybe he ought to have a beer. Might relax him a little, not that he was nervous, exactly— no more than a long-tailed cat in a room full of rocking chairs! Whatever was wrong with him? he wondered, drying his damp palms on the thighs of his jeans. This wasn't a *date,* for pity's sake. It was business. Nevertheless, he left the water glass beside the sink and went to the refrigerator, where he snagged a beer with one hand. On second thought, he grabbed another and wrapped both in a thick kitchen towel.

This way he wouldn't show up empty-handed and he'd get the relaxing effect when he actually needed it. Tucking the bundle under one arm, he went out, calling to his family, "See you later."

He paused on the back stoop to pocket a half-chewed stick he'd seen there earlier, then went, not to the battered old truck he usually drove, but to the late model, double-cab dualie that was both the ranch workhorse and the family vehicle. After placing the wrapped bottles carefully on the seat next to him, he started up the truck, slid in a tape and cranked up the volume. He didn't turn it down again until Danica's cabin came into view. As he parked the truck, she came out of the house, wearing slender jeans that made her legs look a mile long and a coral pink matching sweater set, with the top sweater cropped just below the bust. The dog padded along at her heels.

Winston dug the beers from the protective towel and carried them in one hand to the steps. He plucked the stick from his pocket and tossed it to the dog. Twig snatched it from midair and loped off with it.

"Wet your whistle?" he asked, holding up one of the brown bottles.

A delicately arched brow lifted high, then she swept the bottle from his hand, stepped down and sat on the edge of the porch, her feet on the bottom step. He sat down next to her. The space was just wide enough to comfortably accommodate them both if they were careful with their elbows. She tucked hers in next to her body, held the bottle between her knees and twisted off the top, which she dropped on the bottom step between her feet.

Winston pushed his hat back, decapitated his own drink and dropped the small metal top into his shirt pocket. Lifting the tall bottle to his lips, he took a good drink of the still cold liquid, sighed with sudden contentment and leaned forward, bracing his elbows against his thighs. "Fine night," he said, gazing out over the red-washed horizon.

"Mmm," she agreed, sipping delicately. After a moment, she leaned against the support post of the roof and lifted one foot onto the second step. "It's peaceful out here."

He nodded. "No people." He drank again and expounded, "Funny how it works, isn't it? People just naturally screw up everything, destroy the peace, clog up the works, make all kinds of trouble, but it's people, the people you care about, who make everything in this life worthwhile."

She looked down at that, her free arm crossing over her chest almost protectively. "You have the most irritating way of being absolutely right."

He thought about that, wondering whether he ought to be complimented or insulted, then another thought occurred. "Well, if I'm so right," he asked, "how come you're out here all on your lonesome instead of with the people who should be supporting you now?"

She twisted her upper body so that she could put her head back against the post and took a long drink, grimacing slightly at the end of it. "There aren't any." He wasn't sure he understood that, and it must have showed, for she fixed him with an inscrutable look and elaborated. "I didn't have anyone but Dorinda. Our parents died years ago."

"Oh, hey, I'm sorry."

"Mom was forty-one when we were born, Dad nearly nine years older. I think they'd given up. Then suddenly they had twins."

"Must've been a double shock."

"You might say that," she admitted. "Dad always thought he was too old. Maybe he was. He had a stroke when we were seniors in high school. Mom had just been diagnosed with a serious melanoma, and she always felt that brought it on. She fought the cancer, long and hard, then right after we graduated from college, she let go."

"Man, that's tough," Winston said. "I don't know what Jamesy and I would do without my folks. We almost lost dad in a freak accident a few years ago. Hay baler shot a piece of baling wire about eleven inches long straight into Dad's chest and right through his heart."

She sat up straight again, obviously intrigued. "Good grief! What did you do?"

"We called the doc in Rawlins and headed that way with him, baling wire and all. Doc called the hospital in Cheyenne, and they sent a helicopter to meet us. We intersected about an hour south of here. That pilot set it down right in the road, they loaded him up, and by the time we got to Cheyenne, he was in recovery."

"Thank God you didn't try to pull out the wire!" Danica said.

Win nodded. "We started to. We really did, but none of us had the nerve. He started to do it himself— he was conscious through the whole thing—but we stopped him."

"He'd have died if you hadn't."

"We know that now."

"How is he? Fully recovered?"

Winston wiped a bead of perspiration from the beer bottle. "No, not really. The angle of the wire insured maximum damage. He lost a lot of heart tissue. But we all know that it's a miracle he survived at all, and we're thankful for what we got."

She nodded understanding and said gently, "Dorinda spoke very highly of your parents. She said they were extremely kind and supportive."

He smiled. "They liked her. They like everyone. They even liked Bud. In fact, they were really quite hurt by what he did."

Danica shifted into a more comfortable position. "Tell me about Bud," she said, lifting the bottle again.

He thought a moment, sipped, and began. "He used to come around here during the summers when he was a kid. Ned was his mother's brother, and he never married or had a family of his own, so far as we know, so he was always glad to see Bud. He fairly worshiped that kid, actually, so we didn't tell him some of the stuff Bud got up to. Nothing serious, pranks, mostly, some downright meanness, but he was always real sorry when he got caught."

"I'll bet he was," she muttered, "sorry that he got caught, period."

Winston telegraphed agreement, then went on with his story. "When he got older, he stopped coming around. Ned made all kinds of excuses for him, but we could see that he was hurt. After he died, Bud inherited the ranch. He came back then, full of big plans and big stories about his years on the rodeo circuit. He'd show up again periodically, talking about his latest win. When he came back with Dorinda, I think we all hoped that he'd finally settled down."

Danica sighed heavily and filled in the part of the story to which she was privy. "They met at the rodeo in Mesquite, Texas."

Winston nodded. "I know it. Roped there myself."

She didn't seem surprised. "I begged Dori to take it slow with him, but he was in a hurry to get back to this place. They met and married in less than a month. We found out later that he'd written some hot checks and had to get out of town before they bounced too high."

"Classic Bud," he said. "Slick as grease. When the cattle started disappearing, he was the first one to complain. Even filed a report with the authorities. That's why it took them so long to suspect him."

Danica made a sound of disgust. "Poor Dori didn't have a chance with him, and she deserved so much better."

"He's a smooth operator, no doubt about it," Winston agreed. "Do you know that when the special agent for the cattle growers' association caught him, he was loading the stolen beeves into semis he'd stolen previously from Colorado and North Dakota?"

"So they recovered some of the stock?" she asked.

He spread his hands, showing his own confusion. "Everyone got their stock back but us. I can't tell you how hurt my folks were when he refused to say what he'd done with them. What was even worse was that everyone else lost market-ready steers, which was bad enough, of course, but we lost producing heifers, the very foundation of a herd.''

"Sounds as if he was trying to especially hurt you for some reason.''

Winston furrowed his brow. "Don't I know it. And we were good to him, better than anyone else around here. My folks always felt kind of sorry for him. They said his mom wasn't all that she should have been and that Ned was the only one who really cared about him.''

"Maybe he was jealous of you,'' Danica suggested carefully, but that didn't make any sense to him.

"Yeah, right. The only thing I've got that anyone could envy is Jamesy. I'm thirty-seven years old and still living at home with my parents, for pity's sake. Oh, sure, the ranch will be all mine someday, but what good is that so long as it's just Jamesy and me?''

She tipped her bottle again and asked quite casually, "Why don't you go somewhere else, then?''

He shook his head. "My folks need me here. Besides, this is where I belong. I'm a stockman and proud of it, and there's no better place in the world for it. I was born on this land, grew to manhood here. I expect to die here, and I pray my son follows right along the same trail.''

"Well, then, why not just get a place of your own?''

He shrugged. "No point. My folks were going to build a house close by when I married, but it was pretty obvious from the beginning that Tammy couldn't handle even the everyday stuff, so no one was in any hurry for them to move out. In the end, she was the one to walk away.''

"Tell me about her," Danica said, pulling at her bottle again.

He looked away, hiding his pleasure at this expression of her interest even if it did mean talking about the past. "I met Tammy at the rodeo in Cheyenne."

"Must be something about those rodeos," Danica muttered, and he chuckled because he'd thought that, too.

"I have a deft hand with a rope and thought to try my luck there," he went on. "It was just fun and games at first, but I won, so I kept competing—and for a while I kept winning. Seemed like everywhere I went, Tammy was there, too, so eventually we hooked up. She even traveled with me for a while, and we did have us some high old times, but it got old to me. The competition got stiffer, and the parties got predictable, and I was frankly ready to settle down. So one night in Vegas, we wandered by this little wedding chapel, and I just said, 'What the heck, let's do it.' Next morning I woke up with a pounding headache and a wife. Far as I could see, it was time to come home."

Danica shifted around on the step and copied his position, leaning forward with her elbows propped against her thighs. "What happened?"

He tipped his bottle and admitted, "She hated the place on sight. I think she'd have left within the first month if we hadn't found out she was pregnant. Then, after Jamesy was born, we were fighting all the time. She wanted to go back on the rodeo circuit, and I wanted to stay home with our son. As a sort of compromise, we agreed that I'd take her into Rawlins twice a month for a night out, but I'd lost my taste for it, and she claimed I was no fun. Before long she started going into Rawlins by herself, wouldn't come home for days. I'd have to go looking for her.

"Finally, one day, I realized that she'd packed a bag and taken her things with her. I caught up with her just as she was climbing onto a bus. I said, 'What about Jamesy?' She said, 'He'll be fine with you.' That was almost six years ago. Haven't heard from her since. Didn't even know where to serve the divorce papers.'' He drank again, leaving just a good swallow in the bottom of the bottle.

Hers was only half gone. He saw how the liquid sloshed when she waved her hand. Still, she was definitely mellowed. He saw that in the careless way she leaned her shoulder into his. No drinker here, and he found that he liked that. He wasn't much for the booze himself anymore. On this particular occasion, however, he was glad he'd brought it along.

"Your turn," he said, nudging her with his shoulder. "What's your story? Ever been married?"

She gusted a sigh and ruffled a hand through her hair. "Yeah. Unfortunately." She turned a frank gaze on him and confessed, "You and Dori aren't the only ones who made mistakes in that area."

Somehow that angered him, but deep down where he could keep it easily buried. He wanted to put a comforting arm around her. Instead he asked, "Who was he?"

"A doctor I met during clinicals while I was in nursing school."

"Ah." A doctor, no less. Winston had the definite

feeling that he wouldn't care for the guy, whoever he was.

She nodded and took on a faraway look. "He was handsome and successful and, oh, so charming."

Correction. He definitely disliked the fellow. "So where is Prince Charming today?"

"Probably in some linen closet with his latest conquest," she said bluntly and knocked back a big gulp that made her screw up her face. Definitely no beer drinker. "The first time I caught him, we'd been married just seven months."

"Ouch." Okay, he hated the man, and he was almost pathetically grateful for a good reason to do so.

She nodded, her head bobbing like a cork in water. "I forgave him, that time. We went for marriage counseling. He was contrite, constantly declaring his love. It was almost two years later when I caught him again. This time in his office."

Winston shook his head. How could a man who had the good fortune of being married to a woman like this cheat on her? It didn't compute. "The guy must be sick in the head."

"He's really a very nice man," Danica said. Then she leaned heavily into him and confided, "He has a thing for nurses. I wound up working for him again recently, and he was patting my rear before the first hour was out. You'd think we'd never been married, let alone divorced."

Anger, not at all controllable this time, burst inside Winston's chest and rose hotly upward. Sitting there and allowing it to dissipate to a manageable level required a strength of will that he had not even known he possessed. Finally, however, he was able to lift the bottle, drain it and set it firmly between his feet.

"If you don't mind my asking," he said more tightly than he intended, "how the dickens did you wind up working for the ex who cheated on you?"

She scratched at the label on the bottle with her thumbnail. "I work for a pediatrician named Isling, and he decided that he needed a partner in his private practice, and the one he picked turned out to be Mike."

Mike. "Why didn't you quit?"

"I like my job. Why should I give it up just because Mike works there, too? It's not as if we're at each other's throats or anything."

He found that entirely too amicable for his tastes. "I think I like my situation better."

"Oh, really? You wouldn't change it, not even for Jamesy's sake?"

So much for being right all the time. "Okay," he allowed, "so maybe for Jamesy's sake I'd change it. Not knowing his mother hasn't been easy for him. But I'd keep appropriate boundaries. Working together would be much too close for comfort as far as I'm concerned."

She turned her head and looked at him then, and he fancied that he saw approval there—and maybe something more. Then she spoke and drew his gaze down to her mouth. "You're not what I thought you'd be."

He heard the soft words, even leaned closer to be sure that he heard correctly, but they were sounds without meaning. His mind, his being, was suddenly caught up with the shape and allure of that mouth, with the impulse to taste and press those lips with his own. She tilted her head, and he dropped an arm, circling it loosely about her while leaning closer still. Her chin lifted. He closed his eyes. And then she gasped and leapt up off the porch steps, her free hand going to her hip, fingertips pressing toward the small of her back. He blinked, and then he frowned, while she babbled nervously.

"Will you look at that horizon? Does the sky get that red anywhere else on earth, do you think? You're used to it, I imagine, but I still just want to sit and stare at it sometimes."

Quickly picking through his options, he decided it was best to simply follow her lead and pretend that what had almost happened hadn't. "Yeah, I, um, know what you mean."

She whirled around, saying brightly, "I've been meaning to ask you, where is the store?"

He repeated the question just to be sure he had it right. "Where is the store? What store would that be?"

"You know, the grocery store, I guess, for dog food primarily, but some fresh veggies would be nice, too. All I have here is canned stuff."

That reminded him of something. "I guess you figured out that the refrigerator was unplugged. Dori said it wasn't enough just to turn it off while she was gone. Apparently it was a hang-up of hers, unplugging things, so when she asked me to I came over, moved it out from the wall and unplugged it for her."

She was looking at him like he'd grown a second head. Then she put her hand to her hip again, took a swig of beer and stared off into the distance thoughtfully. When she looked back again, it was as if she hadn't even heard him. "Where did you say that store is?"

He stood and dusted off his seat with both hands, thoroughly disconcerted. "Everything's in Rawlins," he told her. "Whatever you need to get you by until you can go into town, I'm sure Mom can help."

She shook her head. "Uh, no, all I really need is dog food, anyway."

"Are you sure there isn't any on the place?" he asked. "Like everybody else around here, Bud used to buy in bulk. I'd be surprised if he didn't stash several big bags down at the barn. Have you looked there?"

"Uh, no. I didn't think of that, frankly."

"I'll be glad to bring some by tomorrow morning, if you like," he offered. "Dorinda did leave about twenty-five pounds with us."

"Oh, no. I'm sure Twig ate that up long ago. I'll just check the barn, and if I don't find any there, I'll drive into Rawlins."

"Maybe you'd like me to take you into town, show you around a bit," he suggested hopefully.

She squirmed, literally, her weight twisting on the balls of her feet. "Let's, ah, wait and see what I find in the barn."

"I can go look for you now if you want."

"No, no," she refused quickly. "I wouldn't dream of putting you to that trouble. Fact is, I ought to do it myself, get more familiar with the place before I...well, we seem to have gotten way off track here. We were going to talk about the restitution order, and we haven't done that, but then there really isn't much to discuss. You are due restitution, and the court order states that you are to have your pick of forty producing heifers out of ranch stock, so, um, go ahead and pick.''

"Just like that," he said, truly surprised.

"Is there another way?"

"If I was in your shoes," he said bluntly, "I'd want to have a hand in the picking. How do you know I won't make off with your best stock?"

"I trust you." She tossed it out almost flippantly.

That rocked him back on his heels, and it wasn't at all an unpleasant experience. "Okay," he said, smiling. "I'll start looking over your herd tomorrow afternoon. As a courtesy, I want to let Abe Summers know first."

Her brows drew together in confusion. "Who is Abe Summers?"

Surprised, he jerked a thumb over one shoulder. "Neighbor to the northwest. He's been haying your stock. Soon as the case went to trial, the court decided that the Thacker herd had to be protected pending restitution orders, so your beeves have been kept away from the free range. Abe volunteered to see to it because he's the only one for miles around who didn't get hit by Bud."

"Then why didn't you get your stock through him?" Danica asked.

"I considered it," Winston admitted, "but it didn't seem right, putting Abe in the middle of something like that, so I figured to wait for Dorinda."

"And got me instead," she muttered. Then she looked up sharply and asked, "What would you have done if I hadn't shown up here?"

He shrugged. "Guess eventually I'd've headed for Texas."

She shook her head at that and admitted, "Sometimes I don't know what to make of you."

"Well, sometimes I don't know what to make of you," he retorted, slightly stung by what sounded suspiciously like criticism.

To his surprise, she laughed at that. "No, I don't suppose you do. That must make us even."

"Evenly matched," he quipped, and she instantly withdrew.

"I don't know about that."

"We do seem to have a lot in common," he pointed out.

"Yeah, uh, listen, I have to...I mean, thanks for coming by." She switched the bottle to her left hand and stuck out her right. Obviously she didn't have a blasted thing to do, but she was ready to get shed of him. Well, never let it be said that Winston Champlain couldn't take a hint.

He clasped her cool, slender hand in his. "I could bring along a second mount tomorrow in case you change your mind and decide to ride out with me."

She slipped her hand from his and shook her head. "No, thanks. I think I'll leave it to you."

"Okay, then. See you tomorrow afternoon."

She just nodded at that. Then, almost as an afterthought, she raised what was left of her beer and said, "Thanks for the drink, by the way."

"You're welcome. Thanks for the company."

She squinted her eyes and looked away. "Company does seem to be at a premium around here."

"Especially good company," he said softly.

She turned a smile on him, but her gaze did not quite meet his. "Good night," she said.

He had no choice but to return the farewell. "Good night." Bending at the waist, he reached for the bottle he had discarded earlier.

"I'll take care of that," she said impatiently.

He straightened, nodded, fixed his hat more firmly on his head and with a small wave, walked away. It occurred to him that he still had the bottle cap in his pocket, and he lifted a hand to press the spot on his shirt where it rested. The fluted edges bit gently into his skin.

He thought of the moment when they had almost kissed. A moment that might yet be, he wondered, if he were patient? He could be patient. He was good at that. Whether it would pay off in the end or not, he had no way of knowing. She was such a mass of contradictions, this Danica Lynch, angry and suspicious one instant, almost absurdly trusting the next, tilting her chin up to receive his kiss, then suddenly bolting. He didn't quite know what to make of her, but he suspected that, at bottom, she usually exhibited a fine judgment, at least judgment superior to her sister's. He wondered just how much the loss of her twin had affected that aspect of Danica's personality. Patting his pocket, feeling that telltale prick again, he hoped that he would have the opportunity to find out one day.

Chapter Four

She had almost let Winston Champlain kiss her! She could not believe it, even the morning after. What had she been thinking? In truth, she didn't really even have to ask. The thoughts had run through her mind over and over throughout the night. What a nice man. How awful about his marriage. He's a good father. He's a good son. Steady. Responsible. Caring. He had an affair with her sister while Dorinda was still married. And she, Danica, had almost let him kiss her! What kind of an idiot was she to trust a man like that? The same kind of idiot, obviously, who had believed Michael Lynch when he'd said that he'd never cheat on her again. She just didn't seem to learn.

She was still castigating herself for her lapse in judgment the previous evening when Twig began barking sharply out on the porch. Frowning, Danica carried her coffee cup to the screen door in time to see a big, battered black truck pulling a stock trailer rumble into view. Her first reaction was relief that it wasn't Winston Champlain. Her second was that she had no notion who this was.

The truck stopped short of the house at the fork in the narrow road, one branch of which led down to the barn and other outbuildings. The door opened, and a very large individual tumbled out just as the truck lurched into a turn that took it trundling off down toward the barn. Danica stared at the lumbering hulk and realized with a start that it was a woman in jeans and shirt, a very busty one who climbed the slope, skirted the truck and waddled up the steps in astonishingly short order, all the while carrying a rectangular casserole dish the size of a bathtub.

"Honey!"

Danica barely had time to steel herself and stick out her arm, holding the coffee cup at a safe distance, as the big woman—she stood at least six feet tall and could have gone shoulder to shoulder with the average pro football linebacker—lifted the casserole over her head and brought both arms down in a shocking, overwhelming hug.

"We were so sorry to hear about your sister, God love her, and I told Abe, I told him you wouldn't be eating right, bless you, and just feel those bones! Poor little honey!"

Abe? Abe! "You must be Mrs. Summers," Danica exclaimed into the woman's smothering bosom.

Finally the woman released her hold on the mammoth casserole with one hand and stepped back. "Well, bless you, darling, you couldn't have known, could you? Name's Nellie, and I brought you my famous chicken potpie for consolation. Folks around here say they're apt to get sick and suffer loss just to get their hands on my pies, and here you are one of your very own. Abe and Dude'll be along soon as they get those horses unloaded.''

"Horses?" Danica echoed.

Nellie Summers ignored that, if she even heard it. "Where do you want this?" She hefted the monstrous casserole in one hand. "Kitchen, I reckon, and don't that coffee smell good! You can always tell the caliber of a woman by her coffee, I always say. 'Course, that sister of yours, God bless her, didn't drink coffee. Said she preferred a diet cola. I told her, I said it straight, a cold drink don't warm you up on a cold winter morning, and God above knows we got our share of those around here and then some!" With that she suddenly cocked her head, which Danica now saw was wreathed in tight, light brown braids, and inquired sympathetically, "How're you doing, honey?"

"Uh."

With characteristic brusqueness, Nellie Summers abruptly changed the subject. "Let's warm up that coffee and get to know one another."

Danica watched, dumbfounded, while the feminine giant opened the screen door and walked into the house as if she owned it. Dani was still trying to wrap her mind around the thought of horses and glanced in the direction of the barn and corral. The screen creaked again, pulling Danica's attention back to that plump face with its tiny features all crowded together in its center.

"In with you now," Nellie Summers ordered. Danica meekly obeyed and found herself standing in the center of her own kitchen. "That refrigerator was as bare as a board after a sandstorm," the big woman told her with a satisfied chuckle. "How come the pilots aren't lit on your stove?"

"Huh?"

"Pilots. How come they aren't lit?"

Oh. So that was it. Danica shook her head and stammered, "I—I always cooked electric."

Even before the words were out of her mouth, Nellie Summers was setting aside the burner grates and opening cabinets. "You poor thing! I'll just take care of this for you." She'd already found a box of matches and was prying up the top of the stove. She did something under there, dropped the top with a bang and went down onto her knees.

The sight of Nellie Summers with her head, shoulders and bosom crammed into the oven, her big round bottom almost hiding everything else from view, struck Danica speechless. She hadn't known they made blue jeans that wide. When she realized that the woman was wearing black rubber boots with those jeans, her eyebrows leapt straight up into her hairline. Quickly, Danica gulped coffee, anything to stifle the sudden urge to laugh.

After much grunting and groaning, Nellie Summers backed out of the oven, slapped a hand on the countertop and heaved herself up to her feet. "Now," she said, pushing a strand of hair off her forehead, "about that coffee."

Danica blinked, then crossed to the cabinet and pulled down a cup. She'd only discovered the vacuum-packed bricks of coffee in a paper bag high on the top shelf of the pantry the day before and had almost wept with gratitude. Nellie Summers poured the cup full and carried it to the table, where she overwhelmed a chair with her sheer bulk and demanded, "Tell me all about it."

"A-about what?"

"Everything! Anything you want!"

"Well—"

"Me and my mister were that sorry to hear about your sister, God bless her," Nellie interrupted. "Lousy thing that Bud Thacker did to her and to everyone. I told my Dude, I told him, let it be a lesson. If Bud had worked that hard at something honest as he did scheming and stealing, he'd be sitting high and pretty instead of in the pen. And then to die like that." She clucked her tongue, shook her head and sipped her coffee. "There now!" she pronounced, setting the cup down with a plunk. "Didn't I just tell you?"

Danica could only stare, completely lost. The screen creaked, and a fireplug wearing jeans and a black hat stood in the open doorway. "All done, Ma."

"Dude!" Nellie squealed, as if she hadn't known the kid was on the place. "This here is that Lynch woman Winston told us about, the twin to that poor Mrs. Thacker."

Dude didn't so much as glance at Danica. He was younger than she'd first thought, perhaps nine or ten and showing every inclination to match or even surpass his mother in size. "All done, Ma," he said again.

A man clumped up behind him. Abe Summers was a good four inches shorter than his wife but every bit as wide, though in his case all that bulk seemed fash-

ioned from a solid wall of muscle. "All done, Ma,"
he said as if it were a programmed greeting, something genetic with Summers menfolk. This time it was
like a clarion call. Nellie Summers shot to her feet
and hurtled across the room to throw another bear hug
on Danica, who barely had time to set aside her coffee
cup.

"You take care of yourself now, honey. By the
way, that calf is getting a mash of cottonseed, salt
and sorghum. I left the instructions on the lid." She
waddled to the door, her husband and son already
beating across the porch and down the steps. "Oh,
and, that's a damned fine cup of coffee," she said,
pausing to stab a thick finger toward the table.
Dumbly, Danica followed the line of sight to the
barely touched cup. When she looked back, the doorway was empty.

"Lid?" she said weakly. Then in a flash she was
across the room and calling out the door, "What
calf?"

Nellie paused in the act of climbing into the truck
and pointed toward the corral. Then she wedged herself into the cab and slammed the door. Danica
watched helplessly as the Summerses drove away. After a moment, she let out a harsh breath, put a hand
to her head and turned back to the kitchen. It didn't
look any different, she mused, glancing around, but
it had been visited by a whirlwind, nevertheless. For
the first time in a long while, Danica found herself
chuckling.

She went to the stove and turned on the front
burner. It made a sucking sound, then the flame sput-

tered and burst into full bloom. Hot meals. Cold refrigerator. Life suddenly seemed brighter.

Danica thought of the pristine apartment she had let go in Dallas, of the opulent offices where she assisted Drs. Isling and Lynch in their pediatric practice, and the irony of this moment felt all the thicker. Death, she reflected sadly, turning off the burner, had a way of sharpening the smallest pleasures. Life, meanwhile, had a way of asserting itself. Apparently, whether she wished it or not, she had stock to care for—and a chicken potpie in the fridge. She decided she'd better take a look at what Dorinda had unwittingly bequeathed her now. Having noticed a set of keys labeled "Barn" dangling from a hook on the inside of the panty door, Danica retrieved and pocketed them. While she was at it, she might as well look for that store of dog food that Winston was so certain she'd find.

Twig had disappeared the instant that Nellie Summers had shown herself. Now the dog materialized at her ankle. "Let's see what we've got, boy," she said, stepping off the porch. The animal *whuffed* and loped off toward the corral as if it understood exactly where she was going and why.

Situated perhaps fifty yards from the house and shielded by gentle rises in the landscape, the barn and attached corral was a sleek, modern affair of blue sheet metal with white appointments and welded pipe fencing. Dani passed a small well house and another slightly larger, windowless building along the way. A storage shed, perhaps? She'd check into that later. She went straight to the corral and let herself inside via the tall, wide, swinging gate. Twig, meanwhile, slid under the bottom rung and herded a runty, white Charolais calf into one corner by nipping at its heels. The calf bawled mournfully. Danica figured that it had dropped early, or that it had lost its mother and the Summerses had nursed it by hand. Of more interest at the moment were the pair of bays occupying two of the four stalls tucked beneath the overhang of the barn roof.

They might have been a matched set if not for the fact that one of the animals had a blond mane and tail and the other black. Both had their muzzles stuck into empty feed boxes, rumps toward the corral. Spigots emerged from holes in the wall over galvanized water troughs. Talking in a low, soothing tone, Danica let herself into the last stall and ran the tank full while carefully familiarizing herself with the animal and vice versa. To her relief and delight, after some initial sidestepping and suspicious blowing, the big, black-maned gelding tolerated her presence good-naturedly. After a few minutes she slipped out to perform the same tasks next door. The blond was more skittish, but eventually they achieved a meeting of the minds, and Danica let herself out to address those empty feed boxes.

And somewhere there was a lid with some instructions written on it regarding the calf.

She spied three bright green five-gallon buckets in a vacant stall and went to have a look. On the top of each lid in heavy, permanent black marker in a scrawling hand was written "1 can," "2 cans" and "3 cans" respectively. The can in question seemed to be a coffee can which sat on the ground next to the buckets. Seemed easy enough, and it would have been if the sorghum hadn't been sorghum molasses. With only her hands for mixing, she wound up combining the salt and cotton seed in the metal feed bin in the corral, then pouring the molasses over the top of it. The calf butted her out of the way to get to it. She rinsed off beneath the spigot over the water trough, then dried her hands on her jeans, feeling the bump of the keys in her pocket.

Digging the keys from her pocket, she went to the side door of the barn. That door was open but led only into a narrow hall. She felt around for a light switch, found it and flipped on a trio of overhead lights, illuminating four doors. The first opened into a cavernous room crowded with two stock trailers, a battered truck some three decades old and a huge stack of hay bales. Leaving there, she tried the next door and discovered a room full of feed sacks. Immediately inside the door was a stack of paper bags labeled as dog food. *Right again,* Danica mused wryly, thinking of Winston Champlain.

She thought of him again a moment later when she unlocked a well-stocked tack room with no fewer than four saddles and a variety of bridles and other accessories. Several rope cans were stacked along one wall, and she took the top off one to find a well-seasoned lariat coiled inside. A trunk next to the rope cans revealed chaps of various sorts, from crumbly leather to slick canvas.

Everything she needed to ride out with Winston she now possessed. So what good reason did she have for not doing it? Should she trust him? Or was it her own judgment that she should question? Either way, riding out with him seemed prudent, and didn't she owe that much to Dorinda? This place, after all, was all that was to show for Dorinda's life. As her survivor and heir, Dani felt that she should be a good steward of what Dorinda left. By the time she'd looked through the final room with its neatly organized variety of hand tools, she'd made up her mind.

When Winston arrived at Danica's just after lunch, towing a covered, single stall trailer behind the big white truck, the sight that greeted him was both unexpected and pleasing: Danica, decked out in jeans, shirt, denim vest and chaps, boots, gloves and a brown felt cowboy hat. She came out of the house and waved him toward the corral, where Bud's black-maned bay stood saddled outside the fence, the bridle tethered to a post. Winston reached three conclusions simultaneously. One, her home stock obviously had been returned. Two, she had decided to ride out with him today. Three, she made a damned fine-looking cowgirl.

While he couldn't have been more delighted with the turn in events, he was understandably curious about how good of a working hand she might actually be. It wasn't enough just to look the part out here. Anyone hoping to make this his or her life had to have at least an aptitude for traditional cowboying. She and Dorinda both had mentioned growing up on their father's ranch south of Dallas, but it was well known that most ranching in Texas was done from behind the wheel of a truck rather than astride. Here the horse was still the vehicle of choice out on the range. He was uncommonly anxious to see how she handled herself.

By the time he brought the rig to a halt, strapped on his chaps and was ready to unload his big gray, Danica had walked out to the corral, the dog at her heels, and begun tightening the girth on the bay's saddle. Apparently she had performed that task before, as her able actions proved. Moreover, she'd tied a lariat to the saddle skirt, a fact which elevated Winston's mood significantly. Better and better. He just might have found the woman of his dreams.

"So you decided to ride along, after all," he observed aloud, leading his gray to a tether a safe distance away from the bay.

"Might as well," she said as he went back to the truck for his gear. "Got nothing better to do." She adjusted the cheek piece on the bay's bridle and began an expert check of the remaining gear.

"I could think of a few things," Win commented, straight-faced because what he was thinking was probably enough to get him slapped. A rope looped over one shoulder, he wagged his saddle toward the horse with one hand on the horn and the thrust of one leg. Pausing with the saddle braced against his thigh, he straightened the black-and-white blanket spread over the gray's straight back with his free hand, then bent and lifted the saddle into place, stirrups folded up neatly.

"Not on a day like today," she said from behind her bay. "This is the kind of day when you look for an excuse to get in the saddle."

It was true. With blue sky as far as the eye could see, sunshine, temperatures in the low eighties and a cool breeze waving the tops of the grasses, it was a day made for being out of doors, and though Win had been feeling harried earlier, he knew that hard work lay ahead and would happily have ditched it for another sort of exercise altogether, his spirits were suddenly soaring. When Danica swung up into the saddle as easily as if she'd been doing it every day of her life, he could only smile.

"That's a mighty fine cutting horse you're riding there," he told her, hanging the rope on the saddle horn and buckling down a cinch piece. "One thing you can say for Bud, he knew good horseflesh."

"You wouldn't know what he called this one, would you?" she asked.

Winston had to pause in threading the girth to scratch his head. "I'm not sure. He used that horse and the other to steal a lot of cattle, though."

Danica leaned forward and patted the bay's long neck. "Well, I guess we ought to call you Rustler, then."

Winston laughed, put his shoulder into the gray's side and heaved the girth strap tight. "Fitting name," he said, threading it through the ring again. "What about the other one?"

She considered while he shouldered, heaved and threaded again. Finally she decided, "Outlaw. Might as well stick with a theme."

Chuckling, he snugged off the girth strap, lowered the stirrups and tied down the rope. "Nothing I appreciate more than a decisive, logical woman." She rolled her eyes at that, but he smiled as he gathered the reins, put his foot in the stirrup and hauled himself aboard, simultaneously controlling the gray's usual balk.

"What do you call that one?" she wanted to know, moving her horse back to a safer distance.

Win settled himself and put a halt to the gray's sidestepping and circling before he answered. "Grinder."

She reacted as expected, screwing her face up and exclaiming, "What kind of name is that?"

"An appropriate one," he said, adjusting his tension on the rein. "Dad bought this big boy at auction in Colorado just because he's so pretty. Eventually, though, he gave up on ever breaking him and would have sold him if I hadn't needed a project to take my mind off Tammy's leaving."

"Go on," she said, showing her curiosity.

He readjusted his seat and tightened his knees, holding the big gray in place. "I was utterly determined that I was going to train him, but it was slow going, believe me. Dad used to stand outside the corral watching me pick myself up out of the dirt and say, 'Son, that horse is gonna grind your bones into powder if you don't quit him.'"

"Ah."

"Before long, Mom would ask where I'd gotten off to, and Dad would say, 'He's out there working that grinder.' I started thinking of him that way myself, and pretty soon I couldn't seem to think of him any other way."

"Well, he obviously didn't grind your bones to dust, though," Danica argued gently. Evidently the name didn't carry enough romance for her.

"Not yet," Winston allowed, "but it hasn't been ruled out. He's a moody sucker, believe me. When he's on, he's as fine a riding and cutting horse as you've ever seen, and when he's off, it's like dealing with a cranky three-year-old four times your size."

"Let's hope he's on today then," she said, gathering her reins tight.

"Today, he is absolutely on," Winston promised, backing the big horse around. How could he not be on a red-letter day like this?

"Which way?" she wanted to know, seemingly unaware of the pleasure he was taking in this moment.

Win pointed to the east. "If memory serves, there's a draw back that way with a little spring and natural water hole. Ought to be a bunch there."

"Lead on," she said. "You know the place better than I do."

"Okay, but let's give 'em a little head, work some of the frisk off." He rocked the gray into motion, then kneed it into an easy lope, relaxing on the reins a bit.

For a few moments, the animal behaved obediently, but then, true to form, it began lengthening its neck and stride. Winston knew well that if he gave that animal an inch it would take a mile, so he reined in. Danica drew up next to him, her face alight with pleasure.

"What's the matter," she taunted, "can't you stay with him full out?" With that she heeled the bay, which took off like a cannonball, leaving laughter floating on the wind behind her.

It was good, level pasture, and he'd ridden over it before, so Winston felt little compunction about touching his heels to the gray's flanks. He felt even less about laying low and passing her on the flat. Indeed, he had little choice in the matter as the big gray flew like a missile over the ground, cruising low and level. Winston knew well, though, that the big horse would blow himself completely if not controlled, so after a few hundred yards he began reasserting his mastery. After a few dozen more yards, he actually brought the horse to a slow prance. Danica pulled up beside him once more, still laughing.

"Wow! You ought to call him Jet."

"I'm going to have to call him done if we don't get down to business," he quipped.

"Spoilsport," she teased.

Chuckling, he aimed the horse in the right direction. She fell in beside him, and before long they reached the draw. The cattle, fortunately, were not bunched around the water hole but scattered along the rise. Since they were mostly mother cows and weanling calves with a few immature heifers and one young steer in the mix, Win nosed his horse in and around them, getting a look at the stock. What he saw shocked him.

"Holy cow, get a look at that."

"What is it?" Danica asked, easing up beside him.

"The Champ brand. Number sign, one, C. Bud must not have sold off our stock, after all!"

"That means you could get your own stock back."

"No judgment call required," he said. "Frankly, we've been running some fine Simmental, and I was worried about not getting the same quality back or having to raid your best stock to get it."

"This one's calved," she observed astutely.

"Off your Charolais bull, no doubt."

"So what do we do about the calves?" she wanted to know. "There are bound to be more of them.

Doesn't seem fair that I should get them. That means you've been denied the produce of your own heifer.''

"Well, the court didn't take that into consideration.''

"They expected you to redeem the restitution order in a more timely manner, I'm sure,'' she muttered thoughtfully.

"Yeah, well, so I did it to myself,'' he said, shrugging.

"We'll split them,'' she decided, pulling the tie free on her lariat. "We'll gather them all in, look them over and divide them evenly, heifers and bulls alike.''

"You don't have to do that,'' he began, but she brushed that off with a wave of her hand.

"It's fair,'' she said dismissively.

"You're under no legal compunction to split calves with me.''

"Moot point. And I really don't want to argue about it. Now let's get to work.''

If she had any hesitation about putting that bay through its paces, it didn't show. He sat back and let her cut out and drive the heifer and calf away from the bunch, trying to decide whether or not to go along with her notion of splitting any calves produced by his heifers and her bulls. He decided that he would. For one thing, what she proposed was fair. For another, he was finding that he really did like a decisive, logical woman.

"Where to now?'' she asked with a touch of impatience.

He had to grin. It was her ranch, and she'd pretty

much just laid down the law in another matter, but now she deferred to him with surprising ease.

Her brow furrowed. ''What?''

''Nothing,'' he said innocently, looking around for the dog. Spying it, he whistled and brought it to heel. ''Twig will have a better idea where to look next than I do,'' he told her. He gave the dog the command, and it took off to the north. Danica waved her coiled rope at the cow and calf, driving them after the dog. Winston watched her ride for a moment. Darn if her cute little butt didn't look made for the saddle. He put the gray in motion, his grin widening. Yes, sir, the woman of his dreams.

Turned out that the woman of his dreams could work cattle with the best of them. By late afternoon they'd penned seven cows and five calves in the home corral, a good day's work, and Win was feeling on top of the world. When Danica invited him to stable his horse along with hers to save him the trouble of hauling the animal back and forth, he was pleased to accept. A little later, while working silently to put the horses to bed, his empty stomach growled so loudly that Danica looked up from currying her bay.

''Sorry,'' he apologized sheepishly. ''I've worked up quite an appetite here.''

She abruptly dropped her curry brush into the bucket where it was kept and let herself out of the stall, saying, ''You grain them while I put on the casserole.''

''Casserole?'' he echoed.

She shook a stern finger at him. ''It's your fault, so you can darn well help me eat it.''

He could only gape at her. "I don't have the slightest notion what you're talking about."

"I'm talking about Nellie Summers's famous chicken potpie. They showed up with it, the horses and that calf this morning after *you* put them on to me."

Ah. So this was her version of a dinner invitation. It lacked both warmth and finesse, but he couldn't have been more pleased. Grinning, he smacked his lips. "Hot damn! If I know Nellie, she made enough pie to feed your average football team."

"Yeah, well, no team here, just you and me, so you'd better do your fair share and then some," she said tartly.

"No problem," he returned, "and frankly, I think the two of us make a pretty good team."

"Huh." She rolled up her sleeves, not quite meeting his gaze, and warned, "You just remember what I said. I hold you personally responsible. Oh, and don't forget to feed that runty calf. Makings for the mash are in the next stall. Better put him there."

"Yes, boss," he mocked, tugging at his hat brim. She tossed her head and strode away. He watched openly, grinning, and couldn't help noticing that she seemed a little stiff and sore as she walked toward the house. It was still a sweet sight, though, so distracting that the gray tried to take advantage and step on his foot.

"Here, now. None of that," Winston commanded, stepping back and putting away the curry brush. "You behave yourself, and we'll both get fed."

He had to shake his head in wonder at that. First

the afternoon working together and now dinner. Who knew what was still to come? He was humming as he set about his assigned chores. A red-letter day. Definitely a red-letter day.

Chapter Five

Danica yanked a brush through her hair, trying to restore it to some semblance of order, and mentally asked her image just how stupid one woman could get. Riding out with that man today was beyond dumb, but allowing him to stay for dinner had to be right off the scale. Why was it that when she was with him she couldn't seem to remember just what kind of man he really was? How could she forget that he'd had an affair with her married sister? Dori had told her so. Dori had... Come to think of it, Dori had only implied that she and Winston had been involved, and she hadn't really said whether or not that involvement was physical. Might Dorinda have stretched the truth a little? It certainly wasn't beyond her. Wouldn't have been beyond her.

Guilt and shame overwhelmed Danica. Dori was dead, and here she stood trying to justify her own lack of good judgment. Because of a man. A good-

looking, charming man who was doubtlessly just like
all the other good-looking, charming men she had
ever known. And just to make her misery complete,
her thighs and rear end were killing her. Another
"should have." She should have expected such physical ramifications. It had been years since she'd been
on a horse, after all. Funny how it hadn't felt like it
at the time, though. In an odd way, it had felt, for a
while, as if she had come home.

Her eyes filled with sudden, unexpected tears, a
sense of acute loss overriding her other emotions, and
yet it wasn't really the loss of Dorinda this time. It
was...the loss of her grief? No, that didn't make any
sense. Or did it? She couldn't live in the limbo that
grief had granted her forever. Someday she had to get
on with her life. The problem was that she didn't
know quite how to do that. She supposed she'd go
back to Dallas and her job, though the idea held less
and less appeal over time, but what else could she
do? Stay here? For some reason that word *home*
wafted through her mind once more, but she shook
her head. She had no reason to stay here. The squeak
of the screen door alerted her that her dinner guest
had arrived.

Tossing the brush into the sink, she moved down
the short hall and into the kitchen as smoothly as she
could manage, catching the scent of hot chicken potpie as she did so. Winston stood in the doorway, hat
in hand, and smiled at her. Her foolish heart flip-
flopped.

He'd washed up at one of the outside faucets, as
his damp, wavy hair attested. Gone were the chaps
and gloves and heavy shirt. He'd beat the dust from

his jeans and pulled on a clean white T-shirt from somewhere, and still he managed to look like just what he was, a cowboy who'd just come in from the range, a cowboy who, at the moment, needed a shave. She had never found scruffy attractive, but now she found herself resisting the urge to reach out and stroke his jaw with her fingertips. Would it feel as rough, as masculine as she imagined? She couldn't remember ever feeling Michael's jaw except when it was clean shaven. It struck her then, standing there looking at him, that he was just about as different from Michael Lynch as a man could get. She rejected that thought in the next heartbeat. Outwardly, he might be different, but that was all.

Mentally steeling herself against this confusing and unexpected attraction, she snapped, "Well, don't just stand there, come in."

He nodded and stepped carefully over the threshold. The screen clacked closed gently behind him. "Smells great."

In a hurry to get this over with, she motioned brusquely toward the peg in the wall beside the door and turned away, ordering, "Leave your hat there and sit down."

He did that, moving slowly and deliberately as if afraid he might spook her. That irritated her, but in truth that was how she felt, like a nervous filly uncertain whether to bolt, buck or endure. She would, she told herself grimly, endure.

She'd set the table earlier: mismatched stoneware plates, paper napkins, forks, a folded towel to serve as hot pad for the casserole and a bowl of canned peaches. She'd even made a pot of coffee, though it was not her habit to do so this late in the day. Surely she hadn't done that just because Nellie Summers had complimented her coffee. Had she?

"I have coffee, tea and water. Sorry, no beer. Your preference?"

His smile disarmed her. "Black coffee will do me fine, thanks."

She turned away to pour two cups and carry them to the table, trying not to feel anxious. Then, while he sipped and hummed approval, she pretended not to notice. Grabbing a dish towel to use as a pot holder, she opened the oven, bent to remove the casserole and sucked in her breath as the sore muscles pulled and burned.

"Can I help?" he asked, putting aside his cup.

"No, thanks," she said through her teeth, straightening with difficulty under the weight of the dish and the pain of her lower body. As she placed the casserole on the hot pad, he rose and pulled out her chair for her. She tossed aside the towel and allowed him to seat her, biting back a sigh as she eased herself onto the chair. Only then did she realize that she'd forgotten to get out a serving utensil. Groaning aloud, she started to rise again, but he laid a firm hand onto her shoulder and held her in place.

"I'll get it. Which drawer?"

She bit her lip and capitulated. "Try the one to the left of the sink."

"This do?" he asked a moment later, placing a large spatula in front of her.

"I suppose," she muttered ill-naturedly.

He took his seat again and inhaled appreciatively. "I'm starving."

"Dig in," she directed, handing him the spatula.

"Ladies first," he said, reaching for her plate. Cutting into the pie with one hand, he wrestled a large, steamy portion onto the plate that he held with the other. After he set her plate before her, he shoved his own right to the end of the casserole and didn't stop shoveling until the dish was as full as it possibly could be. He closed his eyes, savoring the first bite with obvious relish. "Next to my mama's roast beef," he said, hoisting the next bite on his fork, "there is no food finer than Nellie Summers's chicken pie."

Danica couldn't help a chuckle. "So she told me."

They shared a knowing smile until she realized just how intimate that felt and looked away. He went to work then, proving just how much he enjoyed the food, while keeping a running monologue going about the day's work. Danica had to admit that the pie was delicious, but she didn't enjoy her own half as much as she enjoyed Winston Champlain enjoying his. What she liked most, however, was hearing him praise her work with the cattle. By the time he was done, the pie was half gone, the peach bowl contained only syrup, the coffeepot had been emptied into his cup and she felt a warm inner glow that she hadn't felt in a long time. He drained the last drop from his cup and plunked it down onto the table. Pushing back his chair, he patted his still, miraculously, flat belly and sighed expansively.

"Don't know when I've enjoyed a meal, or an afternoon, more."

Despite her best efforts not to, she smiled. "Well,

I can't take any credit for the meal, but I'm glad if I was of help this afternoon.''

"Hey.'' He lifted his coffee cup for emphasis. "Don't shortchange yourself. That's a darn fine pot you brew.'' He plunked the cup down again, leaned forward, braced his upper body weight on one elbow and said, "To my mind, a beautiful woman who can work cattle and make a fine pot of coffee is as good as it gets.''

A feeling of pleasure so intense that it was embarrassing suffused her, and suddenly she knew that if she didn't put an end to this immediately, she would be in deep, deep trouble, perhaps beyond the point of redemption. Abruptly, she shoved back her chair and shot to her feet. Pain screamed through every muscle, piercing, it seemed, all the way to the bone. She cried out involuntarily, and Winston was beside her in a heartbeat, arms looping gently about her.

"Here now. No sudden movements. You've got to stretch those muscles, warm them up.'' He began easing her toward the living room. "I want you to sit and stretch. I'll show you how.''

"I'm a nurse,'' she snapped. "I know how to perform a sitting stretch.''

"Okay. All right,'' he crooned patiently. "You know then that a warm bath will help limber those tight muscles, right?''

She bit her lip and nodded, gripping his forearm tightly as she slid her feet forward one at a time. When they reached the recliner, she sank down into it gratefully, wincing even though the movement was somewhat easier now. As soon as she was seated,

Winston knelt and began tugging off her boots. "I'm going to run you a hot bath," he said.

Danica glared at the top of his head. "You'll do no such thing!"

He ignored her. "While you're soaking, I'll tidy up the kitchen."

"Absolutely not!"

"Then we'll see how you're getting on." He set aside her boots and rose to his full height, laying a palm atop her head. "I suppose, Nurse Danica, that you have some type of anti-inflammatory handy?"

Moving her head from beneath his warm, heavy touch, she aimed it toward the bathroom. "In the mirror cabinet."

"Stretch," he ordered, walking off in the direction she had indicated.

A few moments later the faucet handles in the bathtub squeaked as he wrenched them on, and water began running into the tub. She tried to feel indignant about that, but the very thought of soaking in a deep tub of hot water was heaven. She bit her lip and began stretching toward her turned-up toes. He returned a little while later with a glass of water and two pills, which she gratefully downed, then he helped her stand. It was easier than expected, and she breathed a sigh of relief.

"Thank you. I'm fine now. I'm sure your family is wondering where you've gotten off to, so you just go on home. I can manage."

"I'll get the kitchen first," he said, moving in that direction, but she grabbed his arm.

"No. Please. I prefer to do it myself. It'll give me

something to do after I get out of the tub, help me keep these muscles loosened up.''

He obviously didn't like it, but he conceded. ''Okay. If you're sure.''

''Yes. Very sure. Thank you.''

He chuckled and laid a hand over hers where it still clutched his arm. Heat radiated upward, spread across her shoulders and flooded downward through her chest to pool in the pit of her belly. ''I'm the one who should be thanking you,'' he said softly. ''You were a lot of help today, and then you capped it by treating me to a fine meal. A man couldn't ask for more. Well, maybe one thing.''

She tilted her head quizzically. ''What's that?''

''This,'' he said, lifting his hand to her face and stepping close.

She told herself that she couldn't step away because of the pain, but in her heart of hearts, she knew that was a lie, and she silently acknowledged as much in the instant before his mouth settled over hers. It was nothing more than a slight pressure at first. A moment later, he moved his head, and his mouth warmed against hers, widening as his arms came around her and pulled her against him.

The room whirled, so that she found herself holding onto him, her hands clasped to his upper arms. Something hot and liquid bubbled low in her body and heated her blood. Her breasts tightened and tingled. Then his tongue stabbed into her mouth and she mindlessly pressed against him, her arms twining about his neck. It was a full-body experience, that kiss, and when he cupped her hips in his big hands and pulled her tight against his pelvis, she knew that it was the same for him.

That knowledge excited her almost beyond bearing. To think that she did that to him! It was heady stuff, heady enough to make her forget all the reasons why she shouldn't be doing this, heady enough to make her want to do more. When he moaned, the sound echoing down into her own chest, she literally shuddered with sensation that bordered on overwhelming and she twisted against him, a desperation building in her. It was only when she went up on tiptoe, rubbing her body against him, that the pain of overworked muscles intruded, making her gasp and jerk.

He immediately backed off, his hands settling at her waist, head lifting. Worried, heated eyes looked down into hers. "You okay, babe?"

Babe. Perspective slapped her in the face. Winston Champlain was calling her "babe," and she had certainly given him reason to think that he could!

"I..." Am an utter fool, she finished silently.

"The tub!" he suddenly exclaimed, wrenching away and hurrying off. Dimly, she acknowledged that water could well be running over the top of the tub onto the floor by now, but that small concern paled in comparison to what had just happened, what she had allowed to happen. She crossed her arms over her chest, humiliatingly aware that her breasts still tingled. How on earth had this happened? She didn't want any man and certainly not this one!

Liar. The word whispered through her consciousness, as shocking as the knell of a brass gong. She gasped again, and suddenly he was there again, arms sliding about her supportively.

"It's okay. I had to let a little water out, but it didn't run over. Let's get you into it now."

"No!" She jerked back. "I—I mean, I'll get into the bath once you're gone."

He seemed a little subdued at that. "Oh. Well, I guess I ought to go, then."

"Yes!" She looked down, greatly relieved.

He cupped her face with his hands and lifted it. Understanding and amusement danced in his smoky eyes. "See you tomorrow," he whispered, bending his head to kiss her once more, lightly this time, with obviously measured restraint that did nothing whatsoever to stop the room from slowly tilting on its axis. When he lifted his head and allowed his hands to fall away, she swayed gently. He stepped back and stared at her until her vision cleared enough to recognize that he felt as dazed as she did.

Finally he rubbed his palms against his thighs and turned away. He paused after lifting his hat from the peg, but then he fitted it onto his head and went out the door. She didn't breathe again until it closed behind him. Then her hand went instinctively to her mouth. Never in her life had she experienced anything like that man's kiss, but, oh, why did it have to be him? Why couldn't it have been some sweet, innocuous fellow like that emergency medical technician she'd dated last year? Or even that shy, stuttering radiologist she'd met at the hospital Christmas party? No, it had to be the very man with whom her poor, late sister had been involved. Oh, God, he didn't consider her a suitable substitute for Dorinda, did he?

She hadn't thought of it before, but that suddenly made an awful lot of sense. Dorinda and she were identical twins, after all. No one who knew them would ever confuse them, of course, but other than the hair, what would he know about that? He didn't really know her, not like he must have known Dorinda. She hadn't considered the possibility that he might have actually been in love with Dori, but now she had to. The notion squeezed her heart like a fist, but she told herself that it was grief and compassion for both Dori and Winston. She did not dare examine the feeling too closely, however. Why should she when it was obvious, for any number of reasons, that Winston Champlain was the very last man on earth with whom she should become involved?

As she hobbled toward the bathroom, gripping the protesting back of one thigh, she swore silently that she would never again let that man near her. Doing so would be tantamount to betraying her own sister, and that Danica could never do. She was going to put this place on the market, dispense of what remained of the herd once Champlain had culled his beeves from it, and return to her life in Dallas. If that thought was accompanied by a welling of tears, well, it had only to do with the pain of her legs and rear end and that of her own foolishness.

He went over early, too early, apparently, for she was a long time in coming to the door. It was obvious from her dress and the disarray of her hair that he had awakened her.

"Sorry," he apologized, "but I'm promised to the Plunketts this afternoon. We all hereabouts pool our labor, you know. That way everyone has time to get the important work done before winter sets in."

"So why aren't some of them over here helping you now?" she asked.

"Well, it was planned for early spring," he explained. "When Dorinda didn't return as expected, I had no way of knowing when she would, so I took it off the table, so to speak."

"Dori didn't call you while she was in Dallas?"

"Nope. Why would she? She didn't have any way of knowing the restitution order had been issued."

"And she didn't leave you a number where she could be reached?"

Something about these questions struck him as odd. "No, why would she? The Summerses were taking care of things around here, not me."

Danica bit her lip and bowed her head, obviously thinking. After a moment she muttered, "She was trying to be sensible, give it time, and obviously I didn't give her enough credit."

"What credit?" he asked. "What are you talking about?"

She shook her head. "Never mind."

He wasn't certain that he should let it go, but daylight was burning, and he had work to do. "How're you feeling this morning? Up to riding out?"

She looked away. "No, I...I'm sorry, but I couldn't possibly climb on a horse again today."

"I understand," he said, trying to keep his disappointment from overwhelming his empathy. "Can I do anything for you?"

"No, no. You just take care of your own business. I'll be fine."

"You really ought to ride tomorrow if you can

manage it," he told her. "Otherwise, you'll have this to do all over again the next time."

"I'll keep that in mind," she mumbled.

"And you'll want to get a fair amount of exercise today, too, or—"

She held up a hand. "I know. I know. I am a nurse, after all. I understand all about muscle conditioning."

He chuckled at that. "Okay, then. See you later." She mumbled something that he didn't quite catch, then stepped back and closed the door.

Winston sighed and hung his head for a moment before turning and heading back to his truck. He'd hoped to avoid this, but he couldn't say that he was particularly surprised. Danica Lynch was obviously a sensitive woman. He had suspected that she would feel guilty about getting on with her life and enjoying things again. It was pure foolishness, of course. Just because her sister was dead was no reason for Danica to stop living, too. Still, he supposed it must be hard for her, being a twin and all. She'd come right in the end, though; he'd seen that much yesterday—and that kiss last night had told him in very eloquent terms how very much she had to offer. His nerve endings still sizzled with it.

Yes, she'd come around, but it wouldn't hurt to move things along a little faster. He grinned to himself, wondering how he should go about it. What he'd like to do probably wasn't the best course. If he could do whatever he wanted, he'd coax her into bed right now, this minute, and wouldn't let her out again until she admitted that the pull between them was enough to warrant very thorough, very deliberate investigation. His smile stretched a little wider as he recalled that kiss again. He'd felt like whistling ever since. Yep, he was definitely going on the prod. The sooner that woman realized what she had standing right in front of her the better.

She'd been dreading the sound of his tread on the porch ever since he'd gone that morning. What she didn't expect was the way her heart lurched and the feeling of gladness that lifted inside her. She tamped it down ruthlessly and hurried to the door, opening it before he could even knock. The sooner met, the sooner gone, she told herself.

"Back already?"

"Yeah, I only pulled in four head, but it's lunchtime, and I want to grab a bite at home before I head over to the Plunketts."

"Well, I won't keep you, then," she said, stepping back and reaching for the door.

"Hold on, now," he said, pulling open the screen.

Why, she asked herself, couldn't she remember to lock that thing? She'd never left the doors open when she'd lived in Dallas.

"No, that's all right. I mean, I'm all right. In fact, I'm just fine. You have work to do," she reminded him, backing up further as he stepped into the room.

"I'm not exactly punching a clock," he said. "It can wait until I deliver my invitation."

Her heart stopped. "I-invitation?"

"Uh-huh, to dinner." She gulped, and he added, "With my family."

Disappointment lanced through her. Not a date then. Good. So why didn't it feel good? "Your family."

"My folks have been wanting to meet you," he said, reaching out a hand to place it on top of her shoulder. She shrugged out from beneath it.

"Oh, I don't know. I wouldn't like to put anyone to any trouble."

"Don't be silly. It would be a special treat for them, especially Mom. She doesn't get much company, you know."

Dorinda winced inwardly, remembering all the kind things her sister had said about Mrs. Champlain, but how could she possibly accept? "I don't think it would be a good idea," Danica hedged, furiously searching her brain for a believable excuse.

He pushed his hat back and folded his arms. "May I ask why not?"

"I, uh, i-it's just that I don't…see the sense in establishing relationships when I plan to leave soon." She smiled, relieved at this stroke of inspiration.

"Oh?"

"I'm only staying long enough to dispose of the property, then I have to go back to Dallas," she expounded.

He grinned with obvious satisfaction. "Well, then you ought to be around quite awhile."

Relief began to fade. "Wh-what do you mean?"

"Danica, this place is two thousand acres of nowhere," he explained patiently. "It takes a special kind of person to make it out here, and they don't just happen by, you know. Besides, if you could get anywhere near what it's worth, it would take a huge infusion of cash from somebody, and the sort with that much money are usually empire building. They'll be looking for places a lot bigger than this, even with your BLM acreage.''

"BLM?"

"It stands for Bureau of Land Management. This place comes with grazing rights to ten thousand acres of public land. Didn't you know?"

"No."

"Well, it does, and that's good, but it's still small by some standards, and The Champ and Summerside leave no room for expansion. Both are larger, working concerns with long, stable histories." He shook his head. "No, I'm afraid the sort of fellow who would dearly love to own and work this place is the last to afford it, and the sort who can afford it, the last to actually want it."

She put her hand to her head, trying to think. Could this be true? "Someone somewhere must want it bad enough to do what it takes to get into it," she argued. "M-maybe I could carry the note."

He shrugged. "That I don't know. If you're serious, though, Dad and I might be able to swing some sort of arrangement. We've talked about enlarging. If you want, we can talk to him about it tomorrow night."

Her eyes widened. He had manipulated that sweetly. "I don't know."

He shifted his weight, hands going to his hips. "Look, why don't you tell me what the problem really is? It's that kiss, isn't it?"

"No!"

His mouth quirked up in a smug grin. "The hell it's not."

She turned away, heart suddenly hammering, mind

in overdrive. It seemed to her in that moment that she had only one option. "All right," she admitted, "it's the kiss." Now the caveat. Turning back to him, she lifted her chin and added, "In light of what happened last night, I think it's best if we keep our distance."

One sandy eyebrow arched. "Do you?" He sounded almost amused.

She ignored that and went on reasonably, warming to the logic and sureness of her position. "It wouldn't be fair."

"No?"

She took a deep breath and went on, careful not to look him squarely in the eye. "I'm simply not interested in you romantically. I'm sorry, but that's just how it is."

"So I just imagined that you were into it last night," he said dryly.

She felt her face color. "Uh…yes, actually."

"I guess you just didn't want to embarrass me by letting me know how much my kiss turned you off."

She gulped, knowing that her heightening color gave the lie to what she was saying. "Something like that."

"In a pig's eye," he said bluntly, stalking toward her.

Truly alarmed, she began backing up again. "Wh-what do you think you're doing?"

"Proving a point."

Before she could react to that, he took one giant step forward and slung an arm about her waist, pulling her to him. His hand cupped the back of her head, holding her still. Even then, she could have moved away had she been able to convince her feet that they should do so. His arm was only lightly looped about her, and the hand at the back of her head exerted no discernible pressure, and yet she stood there like a deer caught in the headlights and watched his mouth descend toward hers. Her eyelids clamped down at the last instant, and then his mouth was on hers, hot and demanding.

Time suspended. Reason absconded. The temperature shot up like a bottle rocket. Her body went on autopilot, naturally seeking that which it craved. The need was amazing, and she had no will, nor even any desire, to counter it. Even last night hadn't prepared her for this. It was as if the thing between them had grown overnight, burgeoning into a ravening monster that consumed every last vestige of her well-ordered determination.

She found herself hanging on to him, arms wrapped about his broad shoulders, body plastered to his while he worked magic with his mouth. His big hands spread across her back, pressing her closer still, and she rebelled at the rightness of it, an echo of reason sounding in some tiny, distant part of her brain. It faded fast, however, and had gone entirely when he suddenly pulled back, looking as stunned as she felt. And then, blast him, he laughed. Laughed!

Humiliation swamped her. Then a smug, know-it-all smile sent her blood pressure right through the roof. "Hey, you're the one who said I'm always right," he told her.

The fact that he was right—again—only added insult to injury. Indignation came to the rescue. "How dare you!" she demanded, leaping back.

"Well, you might say the temptation was simply

irresistible," he told her drolly, "and getting more so."

"It is not!"

"Now, Danica," he warned, tilting his head, "don't make me come over there and prove you wrong. Again."

She wrapped her arms around her chest protectively. "You stay away from me!"

"Sweetheart, I couldn't do that even if I wanted to, which I don't."

She backed farther away, pointing to lend authority to her quivering voice. "I won't have this! I can't."

"Seems a little late for that to me. I mean, we have what we have. Better just to deal with it. Besides, how do you know where this is going? I sure don't."

"I know where you want it to go!" she accused.

"Yeah? And where would that be?"

"To bed, of course!"

"Okay. Seems to me the only real question is which one, yours, mine or *ours?*"

Ours. Something turned over in her chest at the thought. She viciously righted it again. "Don't try to make me believe there's more to this than there is. I know exactly what I am to you, a warm body and nothing more."

He lifted his hat, shook his head slowly side to side, fitted the hat into place again and raked her with a blatant gaze. "I think you underestimate yourself. Be that as it may, I'll be along to pick up your *warm,* or should I say hot, body for dinner tomorrow night, and I won't be taking no for an answer." With that, he turned toward the door.

"Don't you dare leave here until we settle this!"

He sent her a look that could melt the clothing right off her body. "Do you really want me to stay?" She gulped, recognizing the banked fire in his gaze for what it was. "I didn't think so." He smiled then, and there was a world of promise in it. "But you will," he told her. "You will."

He left her gaping like a cod and was fortunately long gone by the time she began calling him names.

PLAY THE
Lucky Key Game

and get

HOW TO PLAY:

1. With a coin, carefully scratch off gold area at the right. Then check the claim chart to see what we have for you — **2 FREE BOOKS** and a **FREE GIFT** — **ALL YOURS FREE!**

2. Send back the card and you'll receive two brand-new Silhouette Romance® novels. These books have a cover price of $3.99 each in the U.S. and $4.50 each in Canada, but they are yours to keep absolutely free.

3. There's no catch. You're under no obligation to buy anything. We charge nothing —ZERO — for your first shipment. And you don't have to make any minimum number of purchases — not even one!

4. The fact is, thousands of readers enjoy receiving books by mail from the Silhouette Reader Service™. They enjoy the convenience of home delivery...they like getting the best new novels at discount prices, **BEFORE** they're available in stores...and they love their *Heart to Heart* subscriber newsletter featuring author news, horoscopes, recipes, book reviews and much more!

5. We hope that after receiving your free books you'll want to remain a subscriber. But the choice is yours — to continue or cancel, any time at all! So why not take us up on our invitation, with no risk of any kind. You'll be glad you did!

YOURS FREE!
A SURPRISE MYSTERY GIFT

We can't tell you what it is...but we're sure you'll like it! A
FREE GIFT—
just for playing the LUCKY KEY game!

Visit us online at
www.eHarlequin.com

FREE GIFTS!

NO COST! NO OBLIGATION TO BUY!
NO PURCHASE NECESSARY!

DETACH AND MAIL CARD TODAY!

© 1997 HARLEQUIN ENTERPRISES LTD. ® and TM are trademarks owned by Harlequin Books S.A. used under license.

PLAY THE
Lucky Key Game

Scratch gold area with a coin.
Then check below to see the gifts you get!

315 SDL DC63
215 SDL DC6X

YES! I have scratched off the gold area. Please send me the 2 Free books and gift for which I qualify. I understand I am under no obligation to purchase any books, as explained on the back and on the opposite page.

NAME   (PLEASE PRINT CLEARLY)

ADDRESS

APT.#   CITY

STATE/PROV.   ZIP/POSTAL CODE

2 free books plus a mystery gift

2 free books

1 free book

Try Again!

(S-R-OS-08/01)

Offer limited to one per household and not valid to current Silhouette Romance® subscribers. All orders subject to approval.

The Silhouette Reader Service™ — Here's how it works:

Accepting your 2 free books and gift places you under no obligation to buy anything. You may keep the books and gift and return the shipping statement marked "cancel." If you do not cancel, about a month later we'll send you 6 additional novels and bill you just $3.15 each in the U.S., or $3.50 each in Canada, plus 25¢ shipping & handling per book and applicable taxes if any.* That's the complete price and — compared to cover prices of $3.99 each in the U.S. and $4.50 each in Canada — it's quite a bargain! You may cancel at any time, but if you choose to continue, every month we'll send you 6 more books, which you may either purchase at the discount price or return to us and cancel your subscription.

*Terms and prices subject to change without notice. Sales tax applicable in N.Y. Canadian residents will be charged applicable provincial taxes and GST.

If offer card is missing write to: Silhouette Reader Service, 3010 Walden Ave., P.O. Box 1867, Buffalo, NY 14240-1867

BUSINESS REPLY MAIL

FIRST-CLASS MAIL   PERMIT NO. 717-003   BUFFALO, NY

POSTAGE WILL BE PAID BY ADDRESSEE

SILHOUETTE READER SERVICE
3010 WALDEN AVE
PO BOX 1867
BUFFALO NY 14240-9952

NO POSTAGE
NECESSARY
IF MAILED
IN THE
UNITED STATES

Chapter Six

She spent the next day in an agony of indecision. If she simply disappeared and didn't return until after he'd come for her and gone again, he would think she was desperate to avoid him, which, admittedly, she was, but she didn't want him to know that because then he'd have no doubt about how very much he affected her. On the other hand, if she actually attended this dinner tonight, she would have to be on constant guard against the inexplicable attraction that she felt for this man. She'd have to tell herself every moment that he was not for her, and only heaven knew if she would listen! The man robbed her of her good sense, and she just didn't know how to deal with that.

After much consideration, she finally realized that her only true choice was to learn to deal with this. The man wasn't going away any time soon, after all, not until his cattle were gathered, anyway, and who knew how long that was going to take? Besides, Dorinda had told her repeatedly how kind his parents were to her, especially his mother, and Dani knew that to refuse the invitation would be the height of ingratitude and churlishness where they were concerned. She had to go, if only to prove to him that she was truly indifferent to his allure, however remarkable it might be. So she would go, but she didn't have to like it.

Nevertheless, she dressed with care, choosing from her meager wardrobe a short, straight, off-white denim skirt with a back split, the coral pink sweater set with the cropped, short-sleeved cardigan and sandals. When Winston arrived around half past six she was so filled with mingled dread and expectation that she was trembling. And she knew exactly whom she had to thank for it. She met him on the porch, wanting nothing more than to get the evening behind her.

"You look great," he said, sweeping his gaze over her. "Nice legs."

"Thanks," she replied brusquely. "Let's go."

"It's not a hanging, you know," he said, voice rich with amusement.

"It's not Christmas, either," she snapped.

He laughed at that, then shook his head. "Man, you are nothing like Dorinda."

She stiffened and glared. "Well, excu-u-se me."

"I'm sorry," he said, instantly looking contrite. "I didn't mean to criticize your sister. I only meant that her happy-go-lucky attitude could be... That is, I'm glad to see that you're more... I meant it as a compliment," he finished lamely.

She didn't know whether she felt more dismay or

delight, but she knew that she had to squelch the latter if she was to survive this evening without making a complete and utter fool of herself. She also knew that Dorinda could be wildly exuberant and patently irresponsible when the mood struck. More than once she had watched her sister skip off to sure trouble, but Dori had always just laughed and gone on her way, no matter what Danica or anyone else had to say about it. Apparently that tendency had not been hidden from Winston Champlain, and apparently he hadn't liked it any more than she, Danica, had.

But no, that couldn't be right. If that were so, then his involvement with Dorinda was even more inexcusable. That would mean that he had used Dori and nothing more, a premise she simply could not accept, though she was not willing to look too closely just now at why.

He helped her into the big, double-cab truck and walked around to get behind the driver's wheel. Danica realized that she was getting the full treatment—the good truck, the compliments. He was dressed as if they were going out on the town, and she had to admit that the man did great things for a pair of creased jeans and a hat. In fact, just looking at him was enough to make her heart trip.

Oh, this would never do. If she was going to make it through this evening, she had to inject some sense of normalcy into the situation. She needed some sort of distraction. Only one presented itself.

"Tell me about your parents," she instructed briskly.

"They're the best people in the world," he said, starting the engine and backing the truck around.

"Mom's like your favorite sweater. She just surrounds you with warmth and comfort that you don't ever get tired of. Dad, now, he's a teaser, but in his way he's more emotional than Mom. He doesn't care any more than she does, it just seems to move him more. I'll never forget the first time he held Jamesy in his arms." Winston cleared his throat and headed the truck off down the lane, adding, "It used to make him uncomfortable, all the emotion, but not any more. I think that changed when he had his accident. It was kind of an emotional time for us all. After, it was like all the caring and fear in us had been exposed, with nothing left to hide. There's a certain freedom in that, you know?"

Danica remembered all the times she had hidden her feelings, for whatever reasons, from those close to her and felt an unusual longing. She could almost grasp the kind of freedom he meant, but the next instant she shied away from it. Exposing her feelings had, more often than not, resulted in nothing except pain for her. That had certainly been the case with Michael and often with Dorinda, too. Perhaps it had been different with her mother. Illness and crisis did have a way of bringing out emotion. She hadn't had the opportunity to express her feelings for her father because of the suddenness of his death, and she did regret that. Still, experience had taught her that it was best to be circumspect when it came to her own emotions. Yet, that longing was very real. She put it aside. It occurred to her that she had become very good at putting aside her feelings, and that thought caused her no little disquiet.

Winston changed the subject, telling her about his

ranch and hers, explaining the BLM plan and how tightly the grazing was scheduled. She listened intently, not because she expected to use the information but because she rather desperately welcomed the diversion. By the time they reached the turn-off to his place, she had learned more about the Bureau of Land Management in Wyoming than she had ever expected to know.

His house did not sit so far back from the road as hers, and the ground around it was flat. The house itself—a neat, two-story wooden structure with a broad, deep porch, white paint with gray trim and a green roof—was surrounded with mature trees and, surprisingly, rose bushes. They parked beside the old truck and, another surprise, a motorcycle beneath a heavy tarp.

"Whose bike?"

"Technically it's Dad's," Winston said, chuckling. "He thought he might be able to work cattle with it, but he never really did more than tear around the countryside. Not since his accident, though. I take it out every once in a while just to keep it tuned and humming. Why? Wanna ride?"

She shook her head. "Not me. I'll bet Dorinda did, though."

He put a hand to the back of his neck. "She brought it up a time or two," he said enigmatically.

"But?"

He shrugged. "Never got around to it."

"I see." She didn't, really, but what did it matter whether or not he had taken Dorinda for a ride on his father's motorcycle?

He got out and started around the truck toward her

door. Quickly, she hopped out by herself, but he still came to her and slid an arm loosely about her waist. "This way."

They walked across the yard and up the steps to the gray-painted porch. The door opened, and a small, plump woman with short, smoky black hair streaked with silver stood there drying her hands on her apron, a smile on her apple-cheeked face.

"Mom, this is Danica Lynch. Danica, my mother Madge." Madge stepped forward, reached up and wrapped Danica in a yeasty hug. A favorite sweater, Win had said, comfortable and warm, an apt description. A tall, thin man with white hair and a truly magnificent mustache stepped into view. "This is my dad, Buck."

"And you're Dorinda's sister," Buck Champlain said, reaching past his wife to swallow Danica's hand with his own wide, long-fingered one. As a type, he and Winston were one and the same, but Win had enough of his mother about him to miss the sharply gaunt, angular look that so defined his father.

"We're sure sorry about poor Dori," Madge said dolefully, stepping back to stand next to her husband. "Such a sad thing, her so young and all, especially after everything she'd been through."

A lump rose in Danica's throat. She managed to speak around it. "My sister spoke most highly of you, ma'am, and I thank you for your kindness toward her while she was here."

"Oh, you mustn't think we did anything extraordinary," Madge argued, ushering Danica into her large, warm kitchen. "You couldn't hardly help liking Dori. She was so bright she fairly lit up a room."

Danica smiled. It was true. Dorinda had a way of transmitting her excitement, and that emotion often held her in its grip, too tightly sometimes, it seemed.

"Yeah, that Dorinda was a vibrant one," Buck said, drawing out the word *vibrant*. "She made you laugh."

"Ever'thing makes you laugh, Grampa," said a small, uncertain voice. Danica remembered with a pang the first time she'd met this child. That was something which still bothered her, and she meant to make up for it as best she could.

"Well, now, why not?" Buck Champlain wanted to know. "I'll take laughing over crying any day. Laughing's a gift, a pure, God-given gift, and you ain't going to be stealing it from me, either, but if you ask nice I just might give it to you." He advanced on the boy, shoulders hunched, fingers wiggling. Jamesy pursed his mouth against a giggle and ducked behind a table chair.

"Now don't you be tickling that boy again, Buck," Madge ordered. "I'll have no such shenanigans in front of company."

"Oh, you won't, will you?" Buck teased, reversing course. He now bore down on her. "Then I guess I'll just have to tickle you."

Madge looked truly alarmed. "Buck, don't you dare!" But Buck did dare. Chasing his plump little wife around the room, he grabbed and tickled and pinched and patted, while she flapped her apron at him ineffectually and the others enjoyed the show, until her scolding turned to laughter that mingled with that of the rest of them and the two wound up embracing in the center of the floor. "You horrible man!'' she exclaimed, but her voice held no rancor, only affection.

Winston enjoyed their antics more than anyone, and it was clear that their play was nothing new to him. He seemed to relish it, in fact, hold it almost, like some sort of talisman inside him, and well he should. It was obvious that their love had endured many years of marriage.

"My roast beef will be ruined," Madge complained, smoothing down her hair and turning to the oven. When she bent to lower the oven door, Buck patted her on the bottom. "Buck Champlain, I swear!"

"You shouldn't give a man that kind of temptation then," he quipped, winking at Winston, who bit his lip to keep from laughing aloud. To Danica he said, "Her roast beef is as fine as her rump."

Madge rose from the oven with a roaster in hand, saying, "Don't you pay him no mind, Danica."

"Dad considers it his purpose in life to entertain us," Winston explained, pressing a hand to the small of Danica's back to move her farther into the room. "Come on, I'll show you around while Mom reshapes his head with that big spoon over there."

Turning, she almost walked right over Jamesy, who had come closer to watch the fun. She stopped to smile at him and say, "It's nice to see you again, Jamesy. Twig and I hoped you'd be over to our place by now for a visit."

"Aw, Twig, he comes over here once in a while," the boy admitted, bowing his head.

"Does he? I'm glad to hear that. I know he misses

you. I was wondering where he gets off to all the time."

"He likes to roam around," the boy told her authoritatively.

Danica disciplined a smile. "I see. We'd still like you to come over to our place, though. Perhaps you could keep me company sometimes, maybe while your dad's gathering cattle on my place?"

"Maybe," Jamesy said with a glance at his father, then he darted off.

"He's shy," Winston explained, ushering her into the living room. "He's always been quiet and a bit of a loner, but he'll warm up presently. He always does."

He needs a mother. The thought popped unbidden into her mind, startling and even frightening her. She looked around the room, denying the idea—and the emotions it evoked—further attention. It was a homey place, much larger than her own, with a pair of comfy couches, several armchairs, occasional tables and a big, black potbellied stove in one corner.

"Oh, my, look at that!"

"Wood's scarce around here," Winston explained. "Better to burn coal or gas, and there's no better source of radiant heat than a cast-iron stove. Dad ordered this one from St. Louis when he built the house, but it's not really as old as it looks."

The rest of the house held similar oddities: a massive, antique grandfather clock in the hallway, an armless rocking chair at his mother's sewing desk in "the east room," a church pew at the foot of his parents' bed, a chandelier made completely of deer antlers over the staircase and a whole collection of old scissors in a display case. Everywhere she looked there were large, framed photographs, some of them quite good. Most surprising and interesting of all, however, was the mural painted on the inner wall of Winston's large bedchamber.

"Who did this?" she breathed, mesmerized by the scene before her. The cattle and riders seemed to actually move, the dust to swirl.

"I did."

"You?"

He shrugged and slid his hands into his pockets. "It's just something I do sometimes. Paint."

She stepped closer, examining the work. "What did you use?"

"Acrylics." He smoothed a hand over the surface. "It gets skinned up sometimes, and I have to touch it up, but I like it better than a canvas, though I putter around with those once in a while, too."

"I had no idea you possessed an artistic side."

He tugged at his earlobe, clearly uncomfortable. "Most cowboys do, but they're usually poets or singers or musicians. Dad, now, he takes photos. You've seen them all over the house, I'm sure." He led her back out into the hall then and to a series of framed color shots that fairly took her breath away.

"These are amazing."

"Aren't they? This one's the Wind River Canyon. This one is Yellowstone, and this one's in the Grand Tetons. You've probably seen them in person."

"No. No, I haven't."

He looked down at her, surprise clearly written on his features. "You can't come to Wyoming without seeing these!" he exclaimed, gesturing at the photos.

"That's like going to the ice cream parlor for the waffle cones and forgetting about the ice cream!"

"I've intended to go," she retorted defensively. "That is, Dorinda and I intended to go." She looked away, swallowed and added, "I—I haven't had the heart to go alone."

"Well, you'll just have to go with me then," he said flatly and began walking back down the hall the way they'd come.

She felt an immediate thrill of anticipation, followed instantly by sheer horror. "I can't do that!"

"Why not?" The question floated over his shoulder, and she hurried to catch up with him, pounding down the stairs on his heels.

"I can't go to those places with you!"

"Of course, you can."

"I—I can't go without my sister!" she tried desperately.

He stopped so abruptly at the foot of the stairs that she nearly bowled him over. Instead, he twisted and caught her against him. Standing above him as she was, they stood nose to nose. "That's plain stupid," he said bluntly. "Your sister wouldn't want that."

Her heart was suddenly pounding so hard that she could barely think, yet the words tumbled out of her mouth, half hopeful, half probing. "How would you know what my sister would want?"

"If she loved you," he said softly, "and she must have, then she couldn't want you to stop enjoying what life has to offer. My impression of her is that she lived too much in every moment to even understand how anyone could refuse to. Besides, I know for a fact that she saw those places with Bud shortly after he brought her here because she talked about it. She must have wanted you to see them, too.''

Was the man always right? Danica thought sourly. She and Dorinda had planned to see those beautiful, majestic areas of Wyoming precisely because Dorinda had wanted to show them to her sister. She would want Danica to see them now without her. ''Maybe I'm just not ready,'' Dani whispered, wondering what this said about his intimate knowledge of her sister. She recalled suddenly that he hadn't even known they were twins.

He smiled sympathetically and tightened his embrace. ''When you are ready,'' he promised, ''we'll go.''

For a moment, the longing returned, yawning inside her so deep and wide that she feared she would never be able to fill it. Then Jamesy bounded into view, heavy boots clumping on the floor.

''Dinner!'' he announced loudly.

Danica instinctively tried to move back from his father, but to her surprise, Winston held her firmly in place and, smiling down at his son, said, ''Lead the way, pard. We're right behind you.''

The boy slid a look between them, then spun on his heel and marched away. Winston turned his smile on her then. ''Dinnertime,'' he whispered. Sliding a hand to the nape of her neck, he tilted his head and lowered his gaze to her mouth. ''Think I'll have my dessert first.''

Why couldn't she move away when he started to kiss her? she wondered, even as her eyes slid closed and her mouth molded to his. A rich poignancy struck her. She wanted this man. Oh, God, how could she want him so? When he lifted his head again, she thought that she had never felt sad in quite this way before. Thankfully, he seemed not to notice, as he escorted her along the central hall to the fragrant, roomy kitchen and the warm heart of his family.

The table fairly groaned beneath the weight of the bountiful meal. It looked like they were feeding a platoon of foot solders. Buck took one end of the rectangular table and Winston the other. Danica sat on Winston's left, next to his mother, and Jamesy sat on his right, leaving the place next to him empty. Buck said a quick grace over the meal and started carving. Once the meat was parceled out in huge chunks so tender they practically melted on the plate, the two men fell to eating like a pair of wolves. It was positively astonishing how much they could pack away. Jamesy did his fair share, too, and that left Madge to keep up a steady stream of conversation about one subject or another, primarily provisioning for the winter.

Buck would stop inhaling food long enough once in awhile to toss in a comical remark, and Winston commented fairly often, too, but it was Madge and Danica who carried the conversation. Everything Danica had heard about Madge was true, but it was that word *comfortable* which most wholly defined her. Meeting Madge was like meeting an old friend whom one remembered only instinctively and yet connected with in a very basic and elemental way. By the end of the meal, which was sinfully delicious, Danica felt surprisingly at ease.

While the men sat nursing coffee cups at the ends of the table, each with his chair canted and his long legs crossed, Madge began clearing away the detritus of their meal, chatting all the while. Danica naturally rose and began helping, so relaxed and caught up in the moment that she almost missed the significant look that passed from son to father and back again. She looked at Winston? "What," she wanted to ask, "was that about?"

His posture and reaction seemed to say, "You're not ready to know yet," for he stood then, getting to his feet with exaggerated laziness, and looked into his coffee cup. "Dad, why don't we go into the living room? There's something I want to talk to you about."

Buck seemed surprised by the suggestion, but then he too rose. "Sure enough, son. Mother, can you girls handle everything in here?"

"If you get out of our way we can," Madge said over her shoulder.

"Done."

Danica watched them exit the room. Why was it that she felt they would be talking about her? Then she realized what was going on. The ranch. Winston was going to approach his father about buying her ranch. Yes, that had to be it. Relieved, she went back to helping Madge clean up the kitchen.

"You can go in with them if you want," Madge told her, smiling as she ran hot water into one side of the double sink. "I don't mind clearing up in here. It's my job."

"Oh, no, I'd like to help."

Madge's smile widened. "That's nice. It's good to have female company. My men are the center of my life, but they are men."

They chuckled about that, while Madge squirted liquid soap into the water and Danica began dropping in flatware. They worked companionably until the last dish was dried and put away, then Madge poured them each a final cup of coffee, put the glass pot in to soak and led the way back to the freshly scrubbed table.

"This has been really nice. I'm so glad Win suggested it."

"Winston suggested it?" Danica echoed in surprise. "I thought you did. I—I mean, he said that you wanted to get to know me."

"Absolutely true," Madge said. "When I mentioned it before, though, Win said you weren't ready. I was purely delighted when he said yesterday that you wanted to come." She reached over and squeezed Danica's hand fondly. "It must have been devastating for you, losing your sister like that."

Danica suddenly felt tears burning her eyes. "Yes. Very much so. Frankly, I didn't think I'd ever..." What she'd almost said suddenly appalled her. She hadn't gotten over her sister's death. She hadn't.

Madge seemed to read her mind. "Well, you never really get over something like that, but it changes over time. I don't know, maybe you just get used to the pain. Somehow, though, you go on and you learn to be happy again. That's what keeps our loved ones from dying in vain—our ability, strengthened by their love and having had them in our lives, to one day enjoy our memories and be happy again."

"Do you really think so?"

"With all my heart."

Danica smiled, feeling lightened, comforted. Other

people had said such things to her, but she hadn't been ready to hear them. "Thank you. All the good things that Dori said about you are true."

Madge chuckled dismissively. "I can't imagine that she talked about me much at all, frankly."

"Oh, but she did. She talked about you and Winston all the time."

"More Win than me, I'm sure," Madge remarked wryly. Then, oddly, her face reddened, and she apologized. "I'm sorry. That was insensitive of me. Whatever Dorinda said, I'm sure she was sincere."

"Well, yes, of course. She was very complimentary."

"Oh, that's nice," Madge said, patting Danica's hand again. "Speaking of nice, Win said you'd been treated to Nellie's potpie. Such good people, the Summerses. You mustn't be put off by Nellie's take-charge manner, now. We call her the human tornado, but at heart she's as sweet and gentle as a kitten."

Danica made some appropriate response, but her mind wasn't really on it. The subject had obviously been changed with a purpose, and she couldn't help wondering what it was. She felt certain that she had heard a hint of criticism in Madge's tone when she'd made that remark about Dorinda talking more of Winston than her. The question was why. Had they actually disliked Dorinda? Or was it something else? Perhaps Madge had disapproved of Winston's involvement with Dorinda, or had the involvement been a figment of Dorinda's overactive imagination? Had Dori pursued Winston rather than the other way around?

She was still pondering the meaning of it all during

the trip back to her place, although she should have
been thinking of other things. For one, while Buck
had been enthusiastic about the idea of absorbing her
ranch into The Champ, he was uncertain that they
could swing it financially. He'd suggested the possibility of a lease, and she'd promised to think about
it. Instead, she was thinking about her sister and Winston Champlain. Telling herself that it didn't matter
was no good, because she simply couldn't stop, not
even when the truck did.

"We're here."

"Hmm?"

Her seat belt suddenly retracted, and when she
turned her head, her nose bumped Winston's.

"I hate for the evening to end," he said softly,
cupping her cheek with his palm. "My folks love
you, by the way. I knew they would. How could they
not?"

He tilted his head and pressed his mouth to hers.
Inside of a minute, she was clinging to him as shame-
lessly as ever. She was so lost she didn't even realize
how low they'd sunk on the seat until his big, hot
hand covered her breast and shot electricity through
her whole body. She was doing it again! Suddenly
galvanized, she jerked upright and fumbled for the
door handle. When the door swung open, she nearly
fell out onto the ground.

"Whoa!" he said, hauling her back in. "Hang on
a minute. I'll come around and—"

"No! No, don't bother." She clambered out and
reached back in for her purse.

He got out and stood tentatively on the other side

of the truck near the front fender. "Are you all
right?"

"Yes, of course," she called brightly, too brightly.
"Thank you for a lovely evening." She quickly
backed toward the house.

"I'll see you tomorrow," he said hopefully.

"Tomorrow," she echoed, running up the steps.
"Bye."

He was still standing there, watching when she
rushed inside and closed the door. This time she
locked it, but she didn't breathe easily until she heard
that truck start up and drive away. Only then was she
sure that she was safe. From herself.

Chapter Seven

He was early again, even earlier than before, and it had less to do with needing to get to work and much more with catching her warm and fuzzy from bed and ready to tumble into his arms. It was half-planned in his head. When she opened the door this time he'd just walk in, apologizing, of course, and then see what he could do about coaxing her back into that still-warm bed. He didn't think he'd really have too hard a time of it, considering the way she kissed him, the way she let him kiss her. True, he'd moved a little too fast last night and spooked her, but she'd had time to get used to the idea now. He liked that she was wary, careful. It meant that this was special, unique.

Standing at her door, he waited and grinned, picturing her shoving back the covers and crawling out of bed to answer his knock. When the door behind the screen opened rather more quickly than he'd expected, he was a little disappointed. When he saw that she was dressed and ready for the day, he was crest-fallen. He was downright hurt when she tossed her head and said almost defiantly over her coffee cup, "What is it now?"

Hurt, he allowed several heartbeats to pass before he could formulate a comeback. "Got any more of that good brew?"

"No, sorry, the pot's empty." She didn't even look over her shoulder to check, let alone offer to make more.

Suddenly he wasn't just hurt, he was angry. "What the hell is wrong with you?"

"Me?" she retorted. "Look, I told you day before yesterday that I'm not interested in…" She waved her hand in circles and looked away. "I don't want to talk about it. Go on about your business and let me get on with mine." She stepped back and closed the door, just like that.

He stared a moment, then he started to go, then he stopped and grabbed the handle on the screen, intending to have it out with her. He could hardly believe that it was locked. She had actually latched the screen! The implications of that caused everything within him to sink. For a long moment he just stood there with his hand on that cool, curved handle, coming to grips with the bald fact of rejection. Finally, as if some autopilot kicked in, he turned and walked away.

She'd held her breath for so long that it had seemed like forever before he'd finally gone away, but instead of feeling the relief she'd expected, she'd felt a kind of shrinking, as if somehow she had made herself smaller by sending him away. It was a stupid thought, of course, and as was so often her habit, she put it away. The restlessness that replaced it was not so easily banished, however, and she did try.

She cleaned out the bedroom and hall closets, bagging up those things of Bud's still there and carefully putting away Dorinda's. It didn't amount to much, but she felt a sense of accomplishment once it was done. Next she reorganized the pantry and the kitchen cabinets, though why was anybody's guess since she had no intention of staying. After that, she moved the furniture and even hauled the area rugs outside to drape them over the porch rail and beat the dust from them with a broom.

Through it all, the vague sense of fitfulness remained, and she wasn't so busy those next couple of days that she did not notice Winston coming and going. She told herself that she was grateful that he no longer came to the house first, just headed off to the corral and barn, saddled up and rode out, but she couldn't quite make herself believe it. When she was sure that he wasn't around, she'd go down to feed the animals and check his progress. He wasn't making much, frankly, and she felt bad about that, so bad she decided that she'd offer her help again, after all. It was childish of her to withhold it when he so obviously needed it. Besides, she reasoned, it would get him out of her hair permanently that much faster.

He didn't come that next day until after lunch. She was out in the yard, bathing Twig in a metal tub she'd found in the barn after he'd come home smelling to high heaven. Twig barked at the sight of the old truck, and she waved, lifting her arm high over her head, but Winston just drove on past. Disappointment mingled with a good deal of embarrassment. She told herself that she couldn't ride out that afternoon anyway. She had to wash this silly dog. All the moisture on her face was not from the dog bath, though.

By the next morning, she'd gathered her courage sufficiently to go down to the corral while he was there. She knew just what she could say, too. All her most pressing work was done now, and she had a few hours to spare, might as well help out. When she got there, she was shocked to find that he was not alone. Another man had accompanied him and was already on horseback. Winston had his own dogs, too. She made her spiel anyway, reasoning inwardly that three could work faster than two, only to be rebuffed.

"No need," he said shortly, busily readying his dun. "Bish and I can handle it."

"Bish?" she queried hopefully.

Winston glanced at the man on horseback in the distance. "It's short for Bishop, neighbor to the southwest of me. If you were going to be around, I'd introduce you. Since you're not..." He let that hang there as he swung up into the saddle and wheeled his mount. Grinder protested, sidling and twisting and tossing his head. By the time Win had the animal fully under control, they were too far away to make any sort of conversation practical. Reluctantly, Danica went back to the house.

It was two full days later before she spoke to Winston again, two long, lonely days during which she read a little, cooked a little, read a little more and took walks, shepherded anxiously by Twig. For some inexplicable reason, the dog had stuck close to the house lately, as if sensing that she needed the companionship, and she was pathetically grateful. In fact, she'd begun to dread leaving the animal behind when she left, and yet she knew that she couldn't take him from this place.

She was sitting out on the porch with Twig when Winston walked up the rise from the direction of the corral and removed his hat to wipe his forehead with his sleeve. He had obviously just come in off the range, still wearing all his gear. He lifted a booted foot to the bottom step, spur jangling, and finally looked at her.

"We're done," he said.

"Already?"

He nodded. "I need you to come down and approve of the take before I drive them over to the home place."

She was still reeling from the news that he was finished gathering cattle. "Uh, o-okay."

He straightened, turned and started walking away. Twig looked at her as if to ask what she was waiting for, so Danica got up and followed. He was standing at the corral, arms folded over the top rail, foot propped on the bottom, when she finally caught up. Two horsemen sat astride their mounts as if waiting for the word to start moving the cattle crammed into her corral. They doffed their hats as she walked past, and she nodded in reply before climbing up on the fence next to Winston. It didn't take long to realize that the forty cattle enclosed in her corral consisted of twenty-five heifers and seventeen calves, some of them obviously bulls. She hopped down again and looked at Winston.

"What's this?"

"Forty head," he said, producing a folded paper. "Sign on the line, and we're done."

She didn't even look at the paper, let alone take it. Instead she folded her arms. "I'll do no such thing. We agreed on forty producing heifers and a fifty-fifty split on the calves."

He took a deep breath as if tamping down his temper and carefully stated, "I'm changing the agreement."

"No, you're not!"

"Look," he said testily, "it's taking too long. These guys have other work to do, and so do I. Sign the damned paper and be done with it."

"It's not fair," she argued.

"Fair or not, we're done."

"I'll help you," she blurted, feeling quite desperate now.

He stared at her as if she was alien to him. "Why would you do that?"

"Because Dorinda would want me to," she said softly. What she didn't say was that she wanted to do it for herself, too, that she had missed him, that she wanted to ride out again, feel a part of this place, these people.

He just stood there, staring, for a long moment, then he abruptly nodded. "Okay. We'll separate your calves, notch their ears, drive the whole lot over to my place to make room for a new gather here. Then we'll drive those over to The Champ, and when your calves are ready, we'll drive them back here. Do you

understand what I'm saying? This is not going to be
a neat operation. It's going to take weeks and weeks.
Some of these calves are new drops, nowhere near
ready to wean.''

She glanced at the corral again. Weeks. Months,
even. Before she could internalize that too clearly, she
looked at him and said, ''Fine.''

His gaze swept over her. Then he rubbed a hand
over his face. ''I don't think you understand what
you're agreeing to. It'll take several half days, maybe
weeks, just to find the other fifteen heifers, and maybe
we'll never find them all! Then the herd has to be
bunched, calves and all and kept separate from any
other. As the calves mature, the bulls have to be cut
so they can be fattened as market steers. In the mean-
time, somebody has to feed and tend them. I can justify the labor because half of the calves will be mine,
but how do I justify feeding your half?''

''I'll feed them,'' she insisted.

''Really? Does that mean you'll just pay for the
feed or actually come over and spread it?''

She thought of driving over to the Champlain place
every day, maybe sitting down to a cup of coffee with
Madge, watching Win come and go, getting to know
Jamesy. The yearning appalled her. She put her chin
in the air and declared, ''I'll do whatever it takes.''

For a moment, he seemed to be trying to look past
her eyes to the thoughts forming in her mind.
''Look,'' he said softly, relaxing his posture somewhat, ''there's another way to go at this. Dad suggested a lease last night, but I've been thinking that
a partnership might be the best way to go. I could
help you really make something of this place, Dani.

We could combine the herds, open the fence lane. Your place is only about a fifth the size of The Champ, but we can work that out. Together, we can make this work.''

Together. Partnership. A permanent partnership. A future. Together. Panic set in. "I—I can't agree to that. I can't tie myself to this place, to you. I just can't.''

She watched those gray eyes harden to granite. "I see. Well, that's pretty plain.''

"I only meant—''

"I know what you meant,'' he interrupted tersely. "I can hear. I speak English. You didn't stutter.''

"I never meant to stay here,'' she whispered plaintively. "I never meant to stay.''

"Fine. Don't let me change anything. Tell you what, you head on back to Dallas. I'll take care of everything here.''

"That's not fair.''

"Life's not fair. We both have ample reason to know it.''

"We have an agreement, Winston,'' she asserted firmly. "I live up to my agreements, and I expect you to live up to yours.''

His mouth firmed into a thin line. "Just remember that I gave you a way out.''

"I can handle my responsibilities,'' she told him, squaring her shoulders. "What time tomorrow do you want to ride out?''

"I'll be here by six.''

Six? She blinked. "In the morning?''

"Well, I don't intend to saddle up at six in the evening.''

She stiffened her spine. "Fine. I'll be ready."

"See that you are." He turned away then and motioned to the men on horseback, calling out, "We'll move 'em through the fence lane to the load-off, then take 'em on the road home." Swinging up onto the dun, which was tired enough not to trouble him this time, he looked to Danica once more. "Better stay out of the way. Some of these cows are rank."

She was in the mood to argue, but she knew that he was right. Again. So she climbed up on the fence and stayed there while he let out the cattle and began hazing them toward the west. It was quite an enterprise, with dogs running around yapping and horsemen swinging coiled lariats at the milling cattle. She stayed there, watching, until nothing remained but puffs of dust on the horizon. Then she jumped down and walked to the house, surprised and oddly pleased to find Twig at her heels. She couldn't help wondering what she had let herself in for. On the other hand, she had weeks, perhaps even months, to find out— and the relief she felt at that fact was truly terrifying.

Win knew that he was letting himself in for a difficult time. She'd had to knock him over the head with it, but he'd finally come to understand that she meant what she'd said. No matter how strong the attraction between them, she simply wanted no part of him. She wasn't the first woman to express the sentiment, obviously, but for some insane reason he'd thought it would be different this time. Unfortunately, his own emotions were not so easily governed. He was constantly torn between wanting to kiss her and wanting to yell at her, which meant that working together was going to be very tough, indeed. On the other hand, he seemed to have a masochistic side, for he couldn't help looking forward to spending time with her. That's why he had to drive real slow after leaving his place to keep from reaching hers before six.

When he pulled up, she was standing on the porch, fully geared, with a cup of coffee in hand. Tossing the remaining brew aside, she set the cup on the porch rail, came down the steps and climbed into the truck. He had to look away to hide his grin. "Morning."

"Sleep well?"

"Fair."

"Me, too."

She had, in fact, apparently slept so well that she'd gotten up at least as early as he had, for the horses stood saddled and waiting at the corral fence when he parked, *both* horses. No one could miss the smug look of satisfaction on her face when he turned to her.

"How on earth did you manage that?"

"Do you know that horse has an awful sweet tooth?" she asked coyly.

"Grinder?"

"Don't forget I've been tending him for a while now. One day I came down with a few stale cookies, and he's been eating out of my hand ever since."

Winston shook his head, amazed. "I knew he liked the occasional apple, and I guess every animal will eat sweets, but I never imagined that was the key to getting him to behave."

"It took a whole dozen hard candies this morning," she admitted sheepishly. "I've almost depleted Dorinda's supply of butterscotch."

Win chuckled. "I guess I better start carrying me some incentive. To think I might have saved my old bones some serious pounding with a few pepper-mints."

"He prefers the butterscotch," she told him, get-ting out of the truck.

Winston shook his head and laughed. Butterscotch. Only Dani could have come up with that. Looked like his start on the day was going to be even earlier than he'd thought.

The work was dirty and grueling, and even at half days the hours were long. At first, they'd ridden in every midday with little to show for their efforts, but eventually they'd culled a baker's dozen of the re-maining fifteen heifers, ten of them with calves. The corral was filling up again. Win stood at the fence looking over the cattle and thought back over the past few days. They had been bittersweet for him, part pain, part pleasure. The cull shouldn't have taken any-where near this long, but despite the early mornings, he couldn't seem to make himself push. In the begin-ning, he'd told himself that it was out of consideration for Danica, but in truth the woman was a natural-born cowpuncher. In fact, she seemed to actually relish the work. He loved seeing it. He very much feared that he loved her, and he was tragically aware that he had no way to hold her.

"Where do you think those last two have gotten?" she asked, walking up beside him.

He shrugged and squinted into the distance. "Could be anywhere, probably somewhere we've already looked. That's the trouble with cows, they've got legs."

She laughed at that, drawing his gaze back to her despite his best intentions. Then she stretched, arms flung behind her, until the buttons on her shirt nearly popped. Winston quickly looked away again, hands coiling into fists. "Well, we'll find them," she said, relaxing with a sigh.

Winston knew he'd reached his limit. Even the pleasure was akin to pain lately. It was just too hard to be with her and not touch her. The bitter had begun to outweigh the sweet. It was time to stop the self-inflicted torture. "I'll find them," he told her roughly. "No reason for you to ride along. Meanwhile, I'll get these out of your hair quick as I can, tomorrow or the next day, for sure."

She had gone very still, so still that he felt compelled to look at her. As if her face was a video screen, emotions flickered across it with the speed of light. He recognized a few of them: confusion, regret, denial, acceptance. "That's fine," she finally said, "but you might as well leave these here until you gather the last of them."

He shook his head. "Naw, better not. I, um, won't be getting by for a few days. Other work."

Several heartbeats later, she said, "I understand. It's okay. I can toss some hay, feed and salt into the feeder a couple times a day." She leaned against the fence, her shoulder brushing his.

Suddenly he knew that he had to get out of there before he said or did something they'd both regret. He backed away and headed for the truck, saying, "I'll send over some fodder."

She hurried after him, silly woman. Didn't she know that he was holding on by a thread?

"Winston, I've been thinking…a-about the ranch."

He stopped dead in his tracks. "What about it?"

"Well, I've been thinking about the partnership you proposed and everything else."

He whirled around. "Have you changed your mind about that? Because we could make it work. You know we could. Just look how well we work together."

For one heart-stopping moment, he thought she was going to agree, but then she shook her head. "No, I…I think it's best if I just sell. I-I'd like to sell to you."

It took real effort to breathe. The disappointment was simply crushing. "I'll speak to my banker," he said brusquely, "but I don't hold out much hope. You might as well see a real estate agent about listing the place."

She bit her lip and nodded. "Who would you suggest?"

"Anyone in Rawlins could help you, but I'd use Tate Collins."

"A-all right. Thank you."

He ducked his head and got out of there, as miserable as he'd ever been. How had he let this happen? he wondered. After Tammy, he really should've known better. After Danica…he couldn't even bear to think about that.

"I'm sorry, Ms. Lynch," the real estate agent said, crossing his hands over the ornate buckle of his western belt. His belly was so big that he could barely

manage it. "We'll do our best, national advertising,
Internet access, and the special financing will help,
but I'd guess we're looking at a year or more to move
the property. Your best bets are to either sell the cattle
and sit on the property for a while or try to make a
deal with one of your neighbors."

Danica tamped down her disappointment and said,
"I've thought of that. Actually, I've spoken to Win,
uh, the Champlains."

Tate Collins nodded. "Abe Summers would be a
more likely possibility. Buck Champlain was injured
a few years back, and they had to take on a short-
term mortgage to pay off the doctor bills. I understand
the payments are pretty high. They might be able to
refinance, but Buck's kind of conservative, and because he's a friend of mine, I know he's worried
about leaving his heirs saddled with debt when he
goes, not that he's planning on checking out anytime
soon, you understand."

Danica smiled wanly. "That's good."

"I could speak to Abe if you want," Mr. Collins
suggested.

Danica wrinkled her nose. "Let's wait on that. The
Champlains haven't refused me outright yet."

"Well, then, you just let me know when you're
ready to proceed."

"I'll do that. Thank you, Mr. Collins." She rose,
and so did he, his broad, littered desk between them.
No taller than she, he had to reach far forward and
actually lay his belly on the desk in order to shake
her hand. Despite that, he projected an aura of com-
petence that inspired trust.

"My pleasure, ma'am. Anything we can do to help, you let us know."

She gathered her handbag tight against her side and backed away a step, but an idea was buzzing around inside her head that just wouldn't go away. "Can I ask you something then?"

"Sure."

"You seem to know about the ranching business."

He chuckled, his belly jiggling. "I should. Grew up on the largest ranch in the state. My brothers still oversee the place."

Her confidence in him grew. "Do you think it would be possible for a woman alone to work a ranch like mine...just until it sells?"

Tate Collins inclined his balding head. "Nope, nor a man alone, either. That's why the ranchers around here team up."

Deflated, she slumped. "I see."

"'Course, you could join the ranchers' association, get their help. Problem is, you don't have any labor to trade."

"That's not true," she said indignantly. "I'll have you know that I'm a darn good cowboy, er, cowgirl. Just ask Win Champlain. I've been helping him round up some stock, and he says I'm a natural."

Tate Collins's round face split into a wide smile. "Well, well, so Win's finally found him one. Good man, that Winston Champlain. I must say that I'm glad he's finally showing interest again. My youngest gal, Nancy, had her cap set for him, you know, but Win's steered plumb clear of women since Tammy walked out. Damn shame what she did to him."

Danica felt a flush of delight, followed instantly by a flood of embarrassment. "Oh, no. You don't—"

"Now, now," Tate Collins interrupted soothingly. "Nan's been married these five years and has two kids to show for it." He winked. "You haven't got anything to worry about. Win'll take care of you. With him in your corner, you'll do fine."

She opened her mouth, realized that further argument would only complicate matters and nodded weakly as she left. Outside on the sidewalk, she paused to try to figure out what it was that bothered her. The notion that Winston Champlain was, once again, entirely correct, proved to be an irritant but not truly unexpected. He'd obviously known what he was talking about when he'd advised her about selling the ranch.

It wasn't hopeless, though. Collins seemed to think Abe Summers might buy her out, but she didn't think it fair to go to him until she had a firm refusal from the Champlains. Perhaps that should've irritated her, but it didn't. She *was* disturbed by the idea that Tate Collins assumed she was involved with Winston—the same way she assumed he'd been involved with Dorinda. In her case, it was only a half truth, but what about Dori?

Had Dori merely imagined Win's interest in her? According to Collins, Winston had steered clear of women. Until now. But then how would Collins know, really? Even if it was the closest town, Rawlins was a long way from The Champ. Did she doubt now, when she hadn't before, just because she so wanted to be wrong?

She didn't know. That was the problem. She didn't know anything anymore, not even herself. How then could she trust her own motives and judgment? How could she trust her own heart?

Chapter Eight

For two days, Danica saw no one. She busied herself with caring for the animals, walks and reading. Sleeping was a problem, for her thoughts and dreams invariably involved Winston Champlain and the question of her future. On the third day, late in the afternoon, almost dinnertime, she was startled by the sound of a car door. It had to be a car, because she recognized too well the sounds of a truck, even above the stereo. She laid aside her book, turned down the music and moved curiously to the door. What she saw through the screen stunned her, so much so that she had to push open the thing to be certain.

"Michael?"

"Thank God!" he said, standing at the foot of the porch steps. "I wasn't sure that old guy I flagged down knew what he was talking about."

She could do nothing more than stare. Michael. Her ex-husband. Here. Coming up the steps and standing on her porch in his expensive pleated slacks and trademark silk T-shirt, that ubiquitous beeper attached to a snakeskin belt, matching Italian loafers on his feet, blond hair artfully tousled, blue eyes sparkling like sapphires. All that was missing was the lab coat and stethoscope. He came toward her, smiling broadly.

"You are a sight for sore eyes."

She let him embrace her. With Michael it was always easier to go along—to a point. "What are you doing here?" she asked against the knob of his shoulder.

"I came to find you, to take you home," he said in that silky, warm, oh-so-intimate voice of his. Fortunately, she had grown immune to that voice long ago. Still very much puzzled, she waited until he released her. He set her aside and, in the same motion, walked straight into her house. It would not occur to Michael to wait for an invitation. She walked in behind him, the screen closing with a clack at her back.

"What happened, Mike? Find yourself with a little time between affairs?" The question was intentionally cynical.

He hung his head, turned, met her gaze with a direct, totally engaging look and said with absolute sincerity, "For the rest of my life I'll pay for my foolishness—willingly, if only you can find it in your heart to forgive me. What I did to you, to us, hurt me, too. Losing you cut me to the bone."

Danica knew just how shallow the good doctor's bones were. "I forgave you the moment I realized how little it mattered," she told him flippantly. "That was—what?—four years ago."

His expression was positively doleful. "Four long years without you."

She had to smile. "I notice you didn't say four long, *lonely* years."

At least he had the good sense not to deny it. Instead he vowed with unctuous gravity, "None of those women could ever replace you."

"Oh, please. For you, Mike, women are completely interchangeable."

He stepped close, took her hands in his. "Not true! Doesn't it matter that you were the only one I married?"

"But not the only one you cheated on," she reminded him.

He closed his eyes, wincing as if the memories were too painful to face. More likely he didn't want her to see the flash of satisfaction that his philandering obviously gave him. "Ah, Dani," he whispered, stepping closer. "If only I could make you understand what you mean to me. Why do you think I convinced Isling to take me on as a partner? I've never loved another woman the way I love you, and I desperately want you back. I tried to tell you for weeks. Then the tragedy of losing Dorinda came, and I knew I had to give you room, but you took off. I've missed you so much, more than you can imagine."

"Office is in chaos, huh?"

"Completely," he admitted with a wry smile. It was the first ring of truth that she'd heard. "But that's not why I'm here," he went on silkily. "I need you, Dani, in every way."

"What you need is a lobotomy if you think I believe that."

He put a hand over his heart. "It's true, I swear. Come home with me. Say you'll take me back."

She brought her face near his, looked him straight in the eye and said, "Not if you were the last man on earth." He reared back, and she went on dryly, "Not even if I was the last woman. Not if we were the only two human beings on the face of the earth. Not even if God Himself—"

"I get the picture," he interrupted disgustedly, hands going to his slender hips. Then the charm oozed forth again, and he vowed, "I'll prove to you that I'm a changed man. Just come home with me."

She shook her head. "I'm not ready to leave here yet."

He glanced around doubtfully, then turned in a circle. "Yeah, I can see how hard this would be to give up. Sheesh. Not exactly the Taj Mahal, is it?"

Danica knew what he saw and simply didn't care. "I think it's rather homey, actually."

"Well, yes, if home is a rough cabin in the woods, minus the woods, of course."

"If you dislike it that much, feel free to go." She waved a hand.

"I'm not leaving here until you agree to go with me," he promised her.

She folded her arms. "Oh, really? Pitch a tent then and get comfortable, because there's only one bedroom here."

Heat flashed in his eyes, and he began slowly stroking his hands up and down her arms. "We could share. Wouldn't that be fun? Think of it, just the two of us."

"As long as no other female wandered by," she retorted.

He gave her an impatient look. "Well, what other alternative is there? I hardly passed another building in the last ninety minutes."

Danica shook her head. "What did you think you were going to do, Mike? Walk in here, sweep me up in your arms and carry me across the street to a five-star hotel?"

He lifted both brows sheepishly. "Seemed like a good idea at the time." She folded her arms. "Okay, I didn't think it through," he admitted, "but now that I'm here…"

It *was* a long way back to Rawlins, she mused, and by the time he got there the motels would probably be full. "I suppose you can sleep on my couch for one night," she conceded.

"The couch?" he echoed disbelievingly.

"You don't think I'm giving up the bed to you, do you?"

He grinned—he had it down to an art. "What about sharing? No strings, if that's how you want it."

"No strings is your specialty, not mine, or don't you remember?"

"Oh, I remember," he said huskily, stepping closer again. "I remember how good it was between us."

She put a hand in the middle of his chest and pushed him back. "And I remember how bad it was. The couch or Rawlins. Makes no difference to me."

He slumped, and the lines of fatigue showed around his mouth and eyes. "This is what I get for driving twenty straight hours to pour my heart out at your feet?"

She rolled her eyes. "Look, Michael, nobody asked you to come. I've told you repeatedly that I'm not interested in rekindling any old flames."

"I know," he said, "but that doesn't stop me from caring about you. Dorinda's death hit you hard. I'm worried about you, Dani."

That, too, had the ring of truth about it. She was quite certain that he cared—as much as he was able and until the next willing woman came along. Sighing inwardly, she made the offer again. "You can stop worrying. I'm fine. And the couch is still available if you're interested."

He sighed, admitting, "It's less than I hoped for, but I just don't think I can get back in that car right now, not tonight."

She understood completely. "It is a long drive. So, come on in and sit down. How did you find me, by the way?" she asked, leading him into the living area.

"Dorinda told me about this place."

She turned at that, alarm bells going off in her head, a tightness in her chest. "When did you speak to Dori?"

"Right after she came back to Dallas," he said innocently, "after her divorce."

Dorinda had never said a word about it. "Where?" Danica asked, trying to think if Dori had ever visited her at the office.

He shrugged and walked over to the sofa, dropping down onto it smoothly. "We had a couple drinks. No big deal."

Big deal, she thought, looking down at him. "And how did that happen?"

He spread his hands and admitted calmly, "I called

her up and asked her to meet me. I needed her advice.''

"About what?"

He clasped his hands together. "You. What else?"

"Dorinda never said anything about it."

He just looked at her, right into her eyes, and she knew then that he wasn't telling her something. She knew, too, that it was probably something she didn't really want to know. Finally, he sat back, got comfortable and rather flippantly commented, "She wasn't much help, frankly. All she wanted to talk about was her crummy ex-husband." He smiled and winked. "She was of the definite opinion that *your* ex was far superior to hers."

Danica shivered, cold suddenly. Dori wouldn't have welcomed a play from Michael, would she? She wasn't that shallow and self-centered. Was she? Danica shook her head, and Michael took it for repudiation.

"Hey," he said. "The guy's in jail. Hello!"

"You're just lucky that spreading it around is a moral, instead of a criminal, offense," she told him smartly.

"I could argue with that if I wasn't so tired," he said. Running a hand through his hair he added hopefully, "And hungry."

Danica sighed. "Lucky for you I haven't eaten dinner yet."

"I'd offer to take you out," he said, "but Rawlins seems an awful long way to go for a hamburger, and I don't think they have much else to offer."

"Oh, Mike," she said, shaking her head, "believe it or not, I think I'm actually glad to see you."

He flashed her that practiced smile again, a touch of smugness about the eyes telling her that he was congratulating himself on his eternal appeal. Oddly grateful for the sudden insight he'd brought her, she let him think what he wanted for the moment.

It was true, after all. Seeing him in the flesh again had crystallized something important for her. This man had nothing in common with Winston Champlain. Looking at him now, she couldn't believe that he had made her afraid of Winston, afraid of herself, afraid of love. But Michael was not her problem anymore. He was the past, little more than a tangible memory, in fact. Her future... She didn't know what the future might hold for her, but she knew that Winston Champlain would be some part of it, even if only as her neighbor and friend.

The issue of Dorinda and Winston was not completely settled in her mind, but it was no longer Winston's perfidies about which she wondered. For the first time since her sister's death, Danica did not automatically shy away from the painful truth about her beloved twin. She hadn't wanted to face it. Somehow, it had seemed easier not to, almost disloyal to remember the bad along with the good, but she couldn't hide from the truth behind her grief forever. She knew that now, and she supposed she had Michael to thank for that, too, as ironic as that seemed. She was grateful enough to put up with him for one night.

"Wash your hands," she instructed briskly.

He shot to his feet, grinning like that infamous cat who ate the canary, and hurried off in the direction she pointed him. She went into the kitchen, washed up at the sink there and took out the makings of a

salad and the frozen lasagna she'd placed in the refrigerator earlier to thaw, all of which she'd purchased
while in Rawlins visiting the real estate agent. The
lasagna was in the oven and she was beginning to put
together a salad when Michael came into the kitchen.

"Let's see. My job was always to set the table, as
I recall."

Figuring it was best to keep him busy, she motioned him toward a particular cabinet door with a
jerk of her head, and he began taking down plates and
glasses. He placed those on the table and returned to
open the drawer containing the flatware, which she
indicated with the point of her knife. It was precisely
then that she heard the sound of a truck.

Michael apparently missed it as he began laying
out the flatware, talking all the while. "Seems like
old times, doesn't it? I've really missed walking into
the house at night and finding dinner on the table—
and you waiting."

Danica barely heard, her attention drawn by the
closing of a truck door. Winston. She laid aside the
knife and wiped her hands on the towel hanging from
the drawer handle, excitement suddenly rising inside
her, gaze glued to the screen door. Just as he stepped
into view, she felt an arm snake about her waist.

"Dani," Michael whispered, "you're ignoring
me." He kissed the curve of her neck, and she el-
bowed him sharply. "Hey!"

"Cut it out!" she hissed, but when she looked up
again, it was straight into Winston's eyes through the
veil of the screen. Her heart dropped like a stone.
Shoving away Michael's hands, she went to the door
and pushed open the screen. "Hello."

His eyes seemed to devour her face, but the next instant they ratcheted upward and hardened.

"Hello," Mike said, stepping up close behind her.

Winston's questioning gaze dropped once more to meet hers. "Obviously, I've come at a bad time," he said.

"No, no," she protested.

"Dinner's not quite ready yet," Michael added helpfully.

"Won't you join us?" Danica asked brightly.

"No, thanks," Winston said gruffly, looking at Mike. "I'm just dropping off some hay for the stock."

"Ah. Well, don't let us keep you," Michael said. His hand landed heavily on Danica's shoulder as he commented to her, "Working the help kind of late, aren't you?"

She shrugged free of him and sent a murderous glare over her shoulder. "He is not hired help. This is my neighbor, Winston Champlain."

"Oh. Sorry." Michael reached past her then, sticking out his hand. "Mike Lynch. Dr. Michael Lynch. Pleased to meet you."

Winston slowly took the offered hand, but his gaze stayed with Danica. She watched the hardening of his jaw, the tick of a tiny muscle in its hollow. "I, um, don't suppose you were just passing through," he said to Michael.

"Hardly," Michael admitted with a chuckle. "A fellow would have to be good and lost to stumble through here." Danica felt her spirits sink further. "Actually, I wandered around quite awhile until some funny old guy stopped and gave me directions. Said his name was Buck.''

"Is that right?" Winston enunciated carefully. Danica closed her eyes, mortified. "Speaking of my father," he went on pointedly, dropping his gaze to Danica once more, "he and Mom sent you a message."

"Oh?" Danica swallowed and forced a smile. "How are they?"

"Busy. They, um, have this get-together every summer, kind of a tradition around here. Everyone for fifty miles around will be there. On Sunday, this Sunday. They wanted me to especially invite you. Should I tell them you'll come?"

"Sunday," Michael interjected, suddenly dropping both hands heavily onto her shoulders. "Oh, she'll be gone by then, at least if I have anything to say about it."

"And you do not!" Danica exclaimed, twisting away.

"Darling, be reasonable," Mike said. "We have to get back to work." He smiled at Winston and explained, "The office is falling apart without her and, frankly, so am I."

Winston shot her a look filled with such accusation that it took her breath away. "Message delivered," he muttered, and turned on his heel. She started after him, only to be brought up short by Michael's hold on her shoulders.

"Winston!"

He didn't even look back. "I'll have those cattle out of your way tomorrow."

"Winston, wait." She pushed away Michael's

hands and ran to the end of the porch, but Winston was already sliding beneath the wheel of the truck. She could only stand and watch the truck drive away, the hay bales still stacked in the bed. When she turned back to Michael, he had that same, innocent, angelic look he always wore when his hands were dirtiest.

"Colorful characters you have around here."

She was so angry she could barely speak. "If you ever do that again, I swear I'll strangle you with your own stethoscope!"

"What?" he demanded innocently, spreading his hands.

"You know perfectly well! You drove him away!"

"I was extremely polite."

"You made him think we were getting back together!"

"I let him know that's what I want," Michael argued. "If he thought the competition was too much for him, that's not my fault."

Knowing that it was useless to argue with him further, she closed her eyes, hands fisting. When she had control of her temper again, she stabbed him with her gaze. "I want you out of here tomorrow."

He smiled placatingly. "We'll see."

"Tomorrow," she reiterated firmly.

He ducked his head, putting on his pitiful little boy look. "What about dinner?"

"You'll get your dinner," she said, tight-lipped, "and breakfast—and that's it. Understand?"

"Whatever you say."

She brushed past him and into the house, knowing that anything she put into her mouth that evening was going to taste like ashes.

* * *

The sun was bright when she woke, still tired from a long, restless night. She'd turned in early just to avoid sitting with Mike, but sleep had not come for many hours, during which she'd gone over and over in her mind last night's incident, wishing she'd said different words, done different things. It was easy in hindsight to know what she should have done and said. At the time, it had not seemed so simple. Everything had happened too quickly. She could still strangle Michael, especially when she walked into her own kitchen and found him cheerfully scrambling eggs while wearing nothing more than a pair of jogging shorts.

"Morning!" he said brightly, turning from the stove to smack a kiss on her cheek.

She jerked back, glaring, and demanded, "Get away from there!"

He turned off the fire, laid aside the spatula, reached for the coffee carafe and took down a clean cup, pouring it full. "Is everyone in Wyoming grumpy in the morning?" he asked, offering it to her.

She took it from him warily. "What do you mean?"

"I mean, your scruffy cowboy nearly took my head off when I answered the door this morning."

She nearly dropped the cup. "Winston is here already?"

Michael leaned into the corner of the counter and shrugged. "Arrived a little while ago."

Raking him with her gaze, she exclaimed, "And you answered the door like that?"

"He woke me. You didn't expect me to sleep in my clothes, did you?"

She closed her eyes, fingers pressed to her forehead. "What did you say to him?"

"Only that you were still asleep."

She could just imagine what Winston thought of that. "I have to talk to him." Placing the coffee cup on the counter, she went out onto the porch. Three trucks were parked at the corral, including the Champlains'. Shading her eyes with her hands, she counted three men on horseback, none of them Winston. Noting absently that the cattle were milling and restless, she searched the area for him. To her surprise, she spotted Jamesy some yards away, playing a game of fetch with Twig, who had gone missing yesterday morning, as he so often did. She looked at the men around the corral and knew that it wouldn't be the best place for the kind of explanations she needed to make to Winston. Leaning against the rail at the end of the porch, she called out to the boy. "Jamesy!"

He looked up and in her direction. She motioned for him to come, and he began trotting toward the house in his heavy boots, the dog at his side. "'Lo, Miz Danica."

"Hello, Jamesy. It's nice to see you again. Where is your father?"

"He's tryin' to catch that bawly calf of yours and pen it so it don't follow them others when we move 'em."

"I see. Could you do me a favor, Jamesy? It's important. Go down and ask your father to come up to the house. I really must speak with him."

"Sure thing. I'll get him. Come on, Twig." The boy turned and trotted off.

Danica went back into the house. Michael was at the table, eating eggs. "Get dressed," she told him bluntly.

"Okay, soon as I finish."

Irritated, she marched over, snatched up the plate and plunked it down again out of his reach. "I said, get dressed. I don't want Winston thinking I approve of you wandering around my house like this."

He stared up at her for a long moment. Then he pushed back his chair, rose and left the table without another word. A moment later, he carried his small suitcase into the bathroom. Danica sighed and went to the counter for her coffee cup, planning what she would say to Winston when he arrived. Michael returned after a few minutes, decently garbed in chinos, a polo shirt and a comfortable pair of leather loafers. Without a word, he moved the plate of now cold eggs back to the end of the table, sat down and began to eat.

Gradually, she realized that a dog was barking in a shrill, frantic manner. An ominous feeling of foreboding came over Danica. She set aside the nearly empty cup again and glanced at the door, but just as she moved toward it, Twig bounded up onto the porch and barked sharply, urgently. She ran to the door. "What is it, boy? What's happened?"

A second figure pounded into view. She recognized the man Winston had called Bish.

"It's the boy! He somehow fell into the corral and got trampled."

Danica gasped and rushed out onto the porch. Michael turned over his chair in his haste to follow. "How did it happen?" she asked, dashing down the steps. Michael leapt over the rail and went straight to the car, where he undoubtedly kept his medical bag.

"Kid climbed up on the fence," Bish explained, falling in beside her, "and then somehow he tumbled over. The cattle were already stirred up on account of Win was trying to catch a calf that had gotten mixed in with 'em. Boy disappeared beneath 'em like a lead weight in water. We turned 'em out right away. Win yelled I was to get you. That's all I know."

They picked up the pace, but Michael passed them on the run, black bag in tow. "He's a doctor," she said, sprinting after him. Twig was long gone already.

"Thank God for that!"

By the time she reached the corral, dodging cattle scattering in every direction, both Winston and Michael were on their knees on the churned, filthy ground, the dog circling anxiously. The boy's treasured hat had been trampled, she noted irrationally. Then she homed in on that small form on the ground between Win and Michael. For one heart-stopping moment, she knew, *knew,* that he was dead. Just like Dorinda. An accident. And this time it was her fault. She had sent him to this. She had sent him after Winston. Then she heard his voice.

"Ow! It hurts!"

She hit the dirt on her knees, a sob bursting from her throat, relief unlike anything she'd ever felt before literally felling her. Winston's head turned, and she saw in his eyes equal measures of worry and relief— and something else, something she didn't recognize until he held out his hand to her. She managed to get up and take the few steps necessary to take that hand. Clasping it tightly she knelt beside him, as close as she could get, and in that moment, she knew it was exactly where she belonged.

Chapter Nine

Danica smiled reassuringly down at Jamesy, who was holding his left wrist, her professional training kicking in as Michael snapped open his bag. "It's okay, sweetie, just be still while Dr. Lynch examines you."

The boy's eyebrows went straight up, even as a tear trickled down his cheek. "H-he's a d-doctor?"

"Yes, he is. I used to work for him."

Michael looked up at her then, surprise in his eyes, but she couldn't imagine why. He immediately went back to checking the boy's limbs, speaking as he worked. "That your dog?"

"N-no, sir, not zactly."

"We sort of share him, don't we, Jamesy?" Danica said, and the boy nodded slowly.

"Any pain here?" Michael asked, feeling the boy's neck.

"No."

Michael moved to the boy's shoulders and began working his way down. "How about here? This okay? And this?" All went well until Michael reached Jamesy's lower right leg. The boy cried out when Michael simply straightened the knee. Michael glanced meaningfully at Danica, and she knew just what to do.

While Michael began gently pulling the boy's shirt from his jeans in order to check his abdomen more thoroughly, again speaking softly all the while, Danica began carefully working off the boot. Fortunately, the boot was large enough to come off easily. The boy still bit his lip and whimpered, but he didn't jerk back or howl as so many frightened children would, increasing both their pain and their own distress.

"You're doing just fine, Jamesy," she crooned, pulling the toe of his sock until the top slipped down over his heel. The ankle was bruised and rapidly swelling. Thank God she had ice in the house.

"Let's have a listen, then I think we can move him," Michael said, plucking his stethoscope from his bag. He gave a cursory listen to the boy's heart, then immediately moved lower. Dani knew that he was listening for sibilance in the lungs, anything that would tell him if air was moving when it shouldn't be. Twig seemed to sense it, too, for he stopped all movement and sat on his haunches. "Sounds good," Mike finally said to Winston, stowing the stethoscope and going for the light. He'd checked Jamesy's pupils before, but he did so now quite thoroughly. "Okay, pal, let's get you to the house, put some cold packs on that wrist and ankle and talk about where we go from here." He gathered his bag and rose, stepping back. "It may be easier for him if you lift him from this side," he said to Winston.

Winston nodded and moved around. Going down on one knee, he slid his arms under the boy's shoulders and knees and carefully lifted him. The dog whined as Jamesy winced, holding his wrist steady with his right hand and stiffening his right leg.

"I'm sorry about the cattle, Dad," he said in a small, pained voice.

"Don't worry about that, son," Winston replied, his own voice understandably husky with emotion as he settled his injured son in his arms. "Next to you, those cattle mean nothing."

"The boys grabbed a few head," Bish said, appearing at Winston's elbow, "and we can start rounding up the rest of 'em right now if you want."

Winston glanced around. "No, that's all right. Just pen those you're holding, then go on to Plunketts'." He began walking toward the house with Jamesy in his arms. Both Danica and Bish paced him. "I'd appreciate it if someone would stop by and let my folks know what's going on, though," he added, striding through the gate.

"Don't worry them more than you must," Danica said, giving in to the urge to grab onto the back of Winston's shirt. "There's nothing wrong here that won't mend."

Bish nodded in obvious relief. "That's good to know, ma'am, real good." He produced Jamesy's hat, which he'd swept clean and punched back into acceptable shape. He tapped Jamesy on the top of the head with the floppy brim, then handed it over to Danica. "One tough kid you got there, Win."

"I know it." Jamesy smiled proudly up at his father through his pain, tears spiking his lashes. "Thanks for your help, Bish, and be sure to tell the other guys that I appreciate their help, too."

Bish nodded and stopped, turning back toward the corral. "Let me know how he does."

"Will do."

They walked several more steps toward the cabin, before Win looked down at the boy and asked, "What were you doing on that fence? You know better than that."

"It's my fault," Danica admitted quickly. Winston turned his head to look at her, never altering his pace. "I sent him for you," she said. "I wanted to explain. Th-things aren't what they may have seemed. You didn't let me tell you last night. I wanted to make certain you understood this morning."

"Understood what?" he asked, the gruffness not quite disguising the underlying emotion in his voice.

She slipped her hand up and over his shoulder. "Let's just say that I'll definitely be at the party on Sunday. Alone. In fact, I expect to be around for some time to come."

Winston's gaze sharpened and then softened just before he looked ahead again. "That's good to know."

She left her hand where it was until they reached the steps, then fell back while Winston carried the boy up onto the porch. Michael stood there, holding open the screen, Twig sitting next to him. Winston passed through, then Danica. Twig slipped in with Mike.

"Take him on into the bedroom," she directed,

moving straight to the freezer. "I'll put together a pair of ice packs."

"I'll grab a glass of water and be right with you," Michael said to Winston. "I have a mild analgesic and an anti-inflammatory I can give him before we head out. I assume the nearest hospital is in Rawlins."

Winston stopped and slowly swung around. "You think he needs a hospital?"

"Not a hospital necessarily but definitely X rays and a thorough exam," Michael said. "I'm guessing the wrist is merely sprained, but I wouldn't take any bets on that ankle. He's probably going to come away from this with a brace and cast, but I wouldn't think more than that."

"Okay," Winston said. "I'll put him down and go get the truck. Dani, have you got a couple of pillows we can use to make him comfortable during the trip?"

"Yes, of course," she answered, working quickly to bag the ice in plastic and wrap it in towels. "I'll get them. We'll be ready to go by the time you get the truck here."

"We?" he said.

She looked around. "I'm certainly going with you." He held her gaze with his for a moment.

"In that case, we better leave a note for my folks."

"I'll take care of it."

Michael looked from Winston to Danica, then down at the floor. "I'll put my bag in the car and follow you in."

"Whatever you say, Doc," Winston told him evenly, carrying Jamesy toward the bedroom, Twig at his heels.

By the time Danica got in there with the ice, Michael had coaxed Jamesy into swallowing several capsules, fashioned a sling for him from a dish towel and stabilized the ankle with a padded wrap, while Twig looked on protectively, front paws braced on the edge of the bed. She wrote a comforting note for the Champlains, telling them to make themselves at home and encouraging them not to worry, then grabbed pillows and blankets and carried everything to the kitchen, where she left the note standing on end between two coffee cups on the table so it couldn't be missed.

Winston pulled up then, and she hurried outside to make a bed in the back seat of the double-cab truck while he went inside for Jamesy. When he came out again, Jamesy in his arms, Mike and the dog at his heels, Danica was struck dumb by the strength and the power of him, not just that of his arms and legs and back but that of his heart and soul, too.

The dog broke the spell, darting down the steps, to the truck and up into the back seat through the open door. "Hey," Danica scolded mildly. "You get out of there."

"No, let him go," Winston said, coming down the steps.

"Yeah, let him go, Dani, please," Jamesy begged as they came toward her. Dani, not Miz Danica. Her heart flip-flopped.

"All right. I don't suppose it'll hurt. But not in the back seat." She reached up and ruffled the boy's hair as they drew up beside her. "I want to ride back there with you, keep you comfortable on the trip."

"'Kay." To her surprise and delight, he reached out with his good arm and looped it around her neck

affectionately. She looked at Winston, saw the smile
in his eyes and felt as if her heart might burst from
her chest. "Let me get in first," she managed, gently
disengaging to duck down and into the back seat. The
dog had already leapt over into the front and seemed
set to watch the whole proceeding.

Danica placed a pillow in her lap. Winston bent
and carefully handed the boy inside. Cradling his
head and shoulders against her chest, she slid across
the seat until she reached the opposite door. Win used
another pillow to prop up the boy's foot, spread a
blanket over him, then carefully closed the door and
quickly got in behind the steering wheel. He patted
the dog. It turned and settled into the seat. Winston
started the engine, then twisted to reach out a hand
to Danica.

"Ready?"

She laid her hand in his. "Ready." Jamesy reached
up and placed his hand on top of Danica's. Winston
briefly closed his own around both.

"Let's go to town."

Releasing them both, he faced forward and shifted
the transmission into gear. After backing the truck
around, he headed it down the rough path at a creep-
ing pace, Michael following in his luxury car. Danica
held Jamesy tight, minimizing the bumps and curves.
Though obviously in some pain, he made no sound,
and once they reached smooth pavement, he seemed
at ease, so much so that eventually he dropped off to
sleep, assisted by Michael's prescription drugs.

Win didn't fool around, neither did he adhere to
the legal speed limit. They fairly flew southward over
the flat, level roadway, passing few vehicles, Michael

keeping pace behind them. They rode in silence for a long while, then Winston glanced into his rearview mirror and said, "After last night, I wouldn't have believed I'd be glad to have that guy around."

"He's a good doctor," Danica told him. "A lousy husband and not much of a human being, frankly, but a good doctor."

"He wants you back," Winston stated flatly.

"Michael always wants what he can't have," she said dismissively, "until he gets it. That's something I learned the hard way and won't forget."

"Do you wish it was otherwise?" he asked in a low voice.

She took a deep breath, thinking about it, and concluded, "Not really. It would be nice for his sake, but it just doesn't have anything to do with me now, and I like it that way." She felt his smile rather than actually saw it.

"Last night," he confessed softly, "I thought..."

"Just what he intended you to," she finished for him.

"I should've stuck around," he said. "I...I made a fool of myself once, and I swore I'd never do it again, but sometimes...sometimes maybe hanging in is worth it, after all."

Danica propped her elbow on the edge of the window sill and rested her head against the palm of her hand. "I can't promise that it will be," she told him honestly. "In many ways, grief still holds me very much in its grip. My whole life has been turned upside down. I never expected to be in this place, emotionally, circumstantially or literally. But I think I'm learning to trust myself again, and maybe, just maybe, my heart is growing wise enough to lead me.''

He shifted in his seat. ''I'd like the chance to point it in a specific direction,'' he said, his voice just slightly more than a husky whisper.

She laughed softly. ''You already have.''

Adjusting the mirror, he gazed into it once more. ''Ought to be an interesting trip. I'm glad I won't be making it on my own.''

She just smiled and looked down at the boy resting peacefully with his head in her lap, her fingertips lightly stroking his hair. Jamesy opened his eyes then and smiled up at her, letting her know that he'd been listening and that while he hadn't understood all they'd said, he'd caught on to the idea that something was developing between them. She winked to let him know that she was pleased by this small show of his approval, and he closed his eyes again, snuggling against her.

The usual pace at the emergency clinic in Rawlins was obviously a lazy, cheerful stroll, but the care could not be faulted. Winston requested that their regular family physician be called, and the man waltzed into the curtained cubicle only a few minutes later wearing denim and boots, the only clue to his occupation the stethoscope dangling from his hip pocket. A large, handsome man in his early to mid-fifties identified as Doc Sheffield, he greeted both Michael and Danica with friendly professionalism, rubber-stamped the orders that had already been issued by Michael and surveyed his patient.

''Aren't you the lucky one?'' he teased. ''When I broke my foot, *I* was the attending physician, and the

only thing female hanging around was the cow that
stepped on it." He leaned over the bed and added
jokingly, "She was a good-looking cow, but not *that*
good-looking." He jerked his head in Danica's direction. Everyone laughed. Danica bobbed in thanks for
a silly compliment that had served to lighten the
mood considerably. Sheffield split a glance between
Danica and Michael, who were standing on opposite
sides of the bed, and asked, "You two wouldn't be
looking to set up practice, would you? We could use
a few more hands around here."

"Afraid not," Michael answered. "I have a pediatric practice in Dallas."

"I might be interested in the right position," Danica put in quickly. "Only problem is that I don't live
close."

Winston shifted so that he was standing next to her
and slid an arm casually around her shoulders, saying,
"Dani's living on the old Thacker place."

The doctor's eyebrows lifted. "Is that so?"

Jamesy piped up then, volunteering, "Dani held
my head in her lap all the way here," as if it might
lend clarification to the doctor's thought processes. As
an afterthought he added, "An' our dog's waitin' in
the truck."

Sheffield turned a purely quizzical look on Winston, who grinned and explained, "Jamesy and Danica are sharing old Ned's dog, Twig. He's pretty protective of them both. We weren't getting off without
him."

The doctor nodded and said to Jamesy, "That dog
saved Ned Thacker's life once. You know that? Must
be good luck, having him around." Jamesy nodded

enthusiastically, winced and hunched his shoulder. "Let's get these clothes off him and have a good look around," the doctor said, suddenly all business, despite the casual bedside manner.

Danica stepped in to help. Michael, too, took part. Winston stood at the foot of the bed, his hand on Jamesy's uninjured leg. The boy received a very thorough examination and was dressed in a soft, cotton hospital gown when the technician came to take him for his X rays. Danica and Winston went along, while Michael stayed behind to consult with Dr. Sheffield. They only got as far as the procedure room door, however, as unnecessary X-ray exposure was strictly forbidden. As she stood against the wall just outside, clutching Winston's hand, Danica developed a new appreciation for the anxiety of parents who waited for their ill or injured children. After what seemed an eternity but had probably been no more than half an hour, the technician opened the door.

"Mr. and Mrs. Champlain? You can come in now, and keep your little boy company while I check the films."

"Oh, we're not…" Danica began, but Winston just thanked the young man and pushed her through the door, murmuring something about details and strangers. Seeing Jamesy lying there in obvious pain on that cold X-ray table was enough to dismiss it from her mind, however. "Honey, are you okay?" He nodded, but his chin trembled. She pulled the sheet from the gurney, which stood against the wall out of the way, and tucked it around him. "I should've remembered to bring a blanket along. These tables are so cold."

"It won't be long now," Winston promised, standing close beside her.

The technician returned within seconds, announcing, "You can go." He maneuvered the gurney into place while Winston carefully lifted Jamesy from the table. Danica took the film folder in hand while Winston made Jamesy comfortable on the gurney, then they both stepped aside while the attendant pushed the wheeled bed out into the hall.

A few minutes later, Michael's initial diagnosis was confirmed. The anklebone was cracked just above the joint, and the wrist was sprained. The doctor ordered a cast and brace prepared. "You're going to be awfully sore and stiff for a few days, young man," Dr. Sheffield warned. "I can give you something to help, but rest is the best cure." He took out his prescription pad and began scribbling. "If someone wants to run down to the pharmacy and have this filled, we'll probably have you ready to go by the time they return."

"I'll do it," Danica volunteered.

"No, no, I will," Winston countered, stepping in to take the form as Sheffield tore it from his pad. "I want to try to call Mom and Dad now that we have news." He winked at Jamesy and said, "I think you'll be in good hands with Nurse Dani, don't you?" Jamesy smiled and nodded. Winston bent and kissed the boy's forehead. "Be back soon."

"'Kay, Dad."

Winston went out, glancing significantly at Danica. The instant the door closed, Michael stepped forward.

"It's time I was going, too," he said.

Danica stared at him in mild confusion. "Uh, if

you were thinking about going back to the ranch, I can't leave just now, but the door's open."

He shook his head. "No. Not the ranch. No reason for that. Right?"

She looked at him and saw understanding in his eyes, understanding and acceptance. "Right," she said gently.

He nodded. "Fortunately I put both of my bags in the car before we left the ranch. I'll tell Isling to start looking for your replacement."

Danica swallowed. The moment of decision had arrived. No, the decision had actually been made, this part of it, anyway, without her putting it into so many words even to herself. The moment to merely acknowledge it had arrived, and she found that she could do it with surprising equanimity. "Thank you, Michael. And thank you for caring enough to try one more time, but mostly thank you for being here when we needed you."

His mouth turned down at the corners, but then he stepped forward and wrapped her in a quick hug before turning to give Sheffield's hand a shake and Jamesy's head a rub. "Behave yourself, cowboy," he said as he swept from the room and, Danica fully expected, from her life.

She was surprised to find just a touch of sadness beneath the relief, but when she looked at the boy again, a very satisfying sort of gladness spilled over and washed it away. Stepping closer to the bed, she took his small hand in hers and smiled. Looked like they were going to be neighbors for a while longer. At least.

* * *

Jamesy slept all the way home. The long, difficult day had taken a toll on him, and the drugs made him sleep soundly. Danica held his head in her lap again and derived a surprisingly intense satisfaction from it. Winston played the radio softly and said nothing, his mien thoughtful and serene. His parents had insisted on meeting them at Danica's, arguing that it would be better for everyone. It would cut an hour from the trip for Dani since she wouldn't have to ride to and from The Champ and also keep Winston from having to manage Jamesy alone should he drop her off first. Plus, the plan had the added benefit of bringing them at least a half hour closer to their grandson. So it was that Dani found herself once more holding a rousing Jamesy tightly as the truck rocked and rolled over the rough lane toward her equally rough cabin. The Champlains both came rushing out onto the porch as the truck pulled up, Madge wringing her hands anxiously.

"He's okay, Mom," Winston said the instant he got out of the truck, "slept all the way back."

"Thank God!" she exclaimed, coming down the steps toward them. "Come on in then. I made something to eat. I figured you'd be empty by now." Danica noticed that Buck stood in the shadows, wiping his face.

Win came around to Dani's side and opened the door. "I hate to move him again," he said in a low voice, "but she tends to cook up a storm when she's worried, and I am bottomed out, frankly."

"He could stay here tonight," she said softly. "You both could."

He pushed back his hat, meeting her gaze levelly. "Could," he said succinctly. "We'll see. Meanwhile, let's get on in."

She nodded, wondering how she was going to accommodate them both. She could put them both in her bed and take the couch, but Jamesy would probably be more comfortable on his own, especially if Win was a rough sleeper. Better to put Jamesy on the couch. And do what with Win? Her heart pounded at the possibilities, which she quickly shoved away as they began easing the boy from the truck. Madge bustled around them, taking the pillows and blankets that Dani bore and whipping them onto the couch and into a comfortable bed in the blink of an eye. Win positioned Jamesy, who then gave his grandparents sleepy hugs, turned his back to the room and slipped off into peaceful slumber again.

"He's on meds," Danica explained. "Nothing major, just enough to help him rest easily until the worst passes."

Buck immediately wanted to know all the details, even though it was obvious Bish had already filled them in, while Madge zipped around putting out sandwiches and cheese soup, apologizing for commandeering Danica's kitchen. Dani just laughed, issued a standing invitation for Madge to take over her kitchen at any time and helped herself to a thick ham sandwich.

"Mmm," she said after biting into the grilled meat. "Where'd you get the ham?"

"It's always wise to go armed," Madge pronounced sagely. "To tell you the truth, I just grabbed the first thing that came to hand. I owe you for the cheese, by the way."

"You don't owe me for anything."

"Yes, I do," Madge said, coming around the table to wrap her arms around Danica. "It was not your fault, and you've done so much."

Dani returned the hug one-armed, feeling lighter and happier than she had in a long, long while. Suddenly she was thinking of banging into the house after school, chattering with Dori, to find their mother waiting with a hug and a smile. "Michael's the one you should thank, really," Danica told her.

"I'm sorry I didn't have the opportunity," Madge said, pulling away.

"You will," Winston said from behind them. Danica turned. "He promised to send me a bill."

Dani first gaped, then she burst out laughing. "That's Mike!"

Winston grinned, a shared knowledge twinkling in his eyes. Buck came in then, and they all sat down to eat. The mood was almost giddy with relief. Madge put back a plate for Jamesy, and they sat around the table drinking coffee and talking until the boy roused, a couple hours later, to complain that he hurt and was hungry. Danica got medication down him while Madge reheated the soup, and everyone moved to the living room, carrying in kitchen chairs so all could sit. The boy ate well and seemed to relish the attention as he told previously unheard details of the accident, how his foot had slipped as he'd climbed over the fence and Twig had rushed to stand over him and drive back the milling cattle, no doubt saving him from greater injury.

"Where is Twig?" Danica asked, suddenly aware that the dog was not with them.

"He slipped off while you all were getting Jamesy out of the truck," Buck answered. "Guess he figured he wasn't needed any more."

Danica shook her head. "That dog is something else."

Winston raised an eyebrow at Jamesy. "Soon as you're up to it, you and I will scrape up a whole big pile of sticks for him, better yet, two, one for here and one for home. What do you think?"

Jamesy smiled and nodded. "We'll get up a whole tree," he vowed, "one itty-bitty piece at a time."

Everyone laughed. Before long, Jamesy grew drowsy again, and Madge and Buck looked at one another. It was Madge who laid a hand on Winston's knee and observed calmly, "You'll be staying here tonight, I reckon. Tomorrow's soon enough to move him again."

Win glanced at Danica and nodded. "Don't worry now. He'll be fine."

"I know he will," Madge said, patting his cheek. "You both will, I think. Dani will see to that."

"Yes, ma'am," Danica promised softly.

Buck got up from the recliner and took Madge by the arm. "Let's go, Mother. I'm plumb tuckered, all worried out."

"We've all had a hard day," she agreed, and moved to the couch to give Jamesy a kiss and hug. "See you tomorrow," she said cheerily, leaving the room.

Winston walked them out while Danica made very sure that Jamesy was comfortable again before he dropped off into deep sleep. As she tucked the covers around him, he kissed her cheek, smiled beatifically and closed his eyes. When she rose and turned, a little misty, Win was standing there watching, the fingertips of both hands tucked into the front pockets of his jeans. After a moment, he slipped his hands free, picked up two kitchen chairs and carried them back into the other room. Danica followed with the third, a sense of expectation growing inside her.

His chairs were already tucked up under the table when she got there, and he leaned against the counter, arms folded, while she placed hers. Only then did he speak.

"I don't know what I'd have done without you today."

She shrugged, feeling a little shy. "Glad I was able to help out, especially since it *was* all my fault."

He shook his head slowly side to side. "No. It was an accident, pure and simple."

She bowed her head at that, then said, "Thank you."

He straightened away from the counter, and she was certain for a moment that he would cross the room, take her into his arms and kiss her senseless. Instead he eased back down again, braced the heels of his hands on the edge of the countertop and said, "We only have one bed."

Her heart leapt straight up into her throat. "I know."

For another long moment he just looked at her as if expecting her to make the proposition they both expected, but just as she opened her mouth to do so, he said suddenly, "I'll sleep in the recliner. It won't be the first time, and I can be near to Jamesy that way."

Disappointment crashed through her, and she heard herself arguing, "That's not necessary." Realizing that she just might be about to make a fool of herself, she quickly backpedaled. "I—I mean, I'll take the recliner."

"No, no," he interrupted. "I won't put you out of your bed."

"I don't mind, really."

"No."

She blinked, recognizing the tone of finality, and gave in. "I'll get you a pillow and blanket."

"Just the blanket," he said. "Can I have the bathroom first? I'll be quick."

"Sure."

He smiled his thanks but then just stood there until she turned and went into the bedroom for the blanket. While she was spreading it over the chair, he returned to the living room, hovering at a distance until she was finished. She checked Jamesy one more time and finally turned to face Winston. "He'll need both meds in about five hours. Otherwise, he'll be in pain."

"I understand."

"All right then. Well, good night."

"See you in the morning." He stepped back as she slipped past him, and he did not move again until she was safely closed behind the bathroom door. Only then did she hear the familiar clump of his boots as he moved to the chair and began preparing to bed down for the night.

She washed and brushed, then slipped into the bedroom and began undressing, ears tuned for his every movement, but only silence issued forth from the liv-

ing area, and ultimately the only sound was that of
her own breathing as she lay in the dark thinking of
the man and boy who, each in his own way, had become so very dear to her heart.

Chapter Ten

Win felt the spoon tumble from his grasp, spilling the contents down his pant leg. "Blast!"

"What's wrong?" He whirled to find Danica standing in the kitchen in flannel pajama bottoms and a big, soft T-shirt. She shoved hair out of her face and looked down at the spoon and small splatter. "What time is it?"

He stooped to retrieve the spoon. "About a quarter past three." He didn't have to look to be certain as he carried the spoon to the sink and rinsed it before returning to swipe a towel over the spill.

"How's Jamesy?" she asked around a yawn.

"Hurting," he snapped and moved back to the counter to begin preparing the medication again. "We both slept through the time he was supposed to take the pill, and when he finally woke me up he was hurting pretty bad, but he couldn't get the pill down that time, said his throat was too dry, so I crushed it, but that tasted so bad, even with water, that he spit it out. I thought if I dissolved it, gave it to him that way, he could manage it, but I spilled it before I got there.'' He was so frustrated that he was mad, and that didn't help anything. His son was still hurting.

She went to the cabinet and calmly took down a small jar of honey, saying, ''Let's try this. Finish crushing the pill.'' While he did that, she took out a soup spoon, rather than the teaspoon he was trying to use, and dipped it into the honey, cleaning the excess from the back on the edge of the jar. ''Now the pill powder.'' Using his fingertip, he pushed the powder from the bowl of the small spoon onto the thin layer of honey in the tablespoon. ''Let me have that,'' she said, taking the small spoon from his hand. Next she dipped that spoon into the jar and dribbled a little honey on top of the crushed pill. ''Bring a glass of lukewarm water,'' she instructed, carrying the tablespoon.

He ran the water, adjusting the temperature from cold to lukewarm, into a glass and followed in his stocking feet. By the time he reached them, she had already convinced Jamesy to take the big spoon into his mouth. His eyes widened at the taste of honey. Only after he swallowed did the bitter taste of the pill hit him. Winston handed over the water, and Danica helped Jamesy drink it down. Finally, the boy lay back on the pillow, his face drawn and pale, and offered them a wan smile.

Winston's heart squeezed inside his chest. He hadn't felt this helpless even when it had first happened. At that time, his entire being had been focused on remaining calm and assessing the damage in order to rescue his boy. Now all he could do was agonize and hover. He hated it. Making him feel even more useless, Danica sat down on the floor next to the couch and began stroking Jamesy's hair, something the boy would never have allowed Winston to do but seemed to relish when she did. After a bit, however, Jamesy seemed to relax, and Winston breathed a mental sigh of relief.

"I'm sorry I woke you," he said to Danica, "but I couldn't have gotten that pill down him otherwise."

"Pills are always problematic for children," Danica explained, looking up at him, "but they provide the most exact dosage and, therefore, the most relief with the least risk. Liquids spill, and well-meaning parents try to compensate and sometimes wind up overdosing. So when a child demonstrates the ability to swallow the pills, doctors like to prescribe them. Unfortunately, they don't always go down as easily as we might hope."

"If he hadn't missed the dose," Winston said bitterly, "he wouldn't have been in so much pain and wouldn't have had so much trouble getting it down. I should've set the alarm on my watch, but I didn't think I'd sleep."

"He slept through it, too," she pointed out gently. "Lots of parents don't want to wake a sleeping child to administer medication, and sometimes that's okay, but sometimes it's not. We can't always predict."

"Can I go to the bathroom, please," Jamesy interrupted.

Danica got up off the floor, saying, "Sounds like a daddy job to me."

Winston felt a rush of gratitude. She was right, of

course. This was one service Jamesy would definitely prefer that his dad perform. He folded back the covers and carefully scooped up the boy. Jamesy managed it well, all the way through to the hand-washing. By the time he was tucked back into his makeshift bed, he seemed entirely comfortable again, save for the inconvenience of brace and cast. Within moments, he was sleeping peacefully once more.

Winston sat down on the edge of the recliner and put his face in his hands. He felt as shaky as a newborn colt. Danica laid a hand on his shoulder, and her knee nudged his. He'd told himself that he was going to go slow with her, not take a chance on scaring her off again, but in that moment he needed nothing more than to hold and be held, and that he needed fiercely.

Looking up, he slid his arms around her waist. Her own slipped about his shoulders, and she leaned into him. He laid his face against her midriff beneath her breasts and closed his eyes, smelling the bed-warm, womanly perfume of her. How good she felt! How wonderful it was to simply hold and be held, but how easy it would be to want more. For her, too, apparently, as she lightly stroked the back of his head and softly urged, "Come with me now. You need to relax and rest. Jamesy will sleep peacefully until morning, I promise."

He inhaled, pulling as much of her into his lungs as he could, and felt the need in him turn from comfort to desire. He lifted his head, nuzzling her breast lightly, letting her know that if he came with her now it would not be a simple matter of rest and relaxation. She caught her breath, then reached back to take both his hands in hers.

"Come on."

Stepping away, she pulled at him gently, her gaze openly pleading. He rose slowly, aware of an intensely masculine power rushing through him. She turned, keeping one of his hands in hers, and led him into the hall. He stopped her there in the shadows, the light from the kitchen spilling diagonally across the end of the hallway and into the living area, where it gradually diffused. Taking her face in his hands, he bent his head to hers, thrilling when she went up on tiptoe to eagerly meet him. He felt that power surge again, compelling him to push her against the wall and press into the sweetness of that soft body. The lush weight of her unfettered breasts beneath her T-shirt surprised and inflamed him. He shoved a hand between them, cupping and covering the heavy mound. She moaned into his mouth, her arms tight about his neck, and he plunged his tongue into her, desperation clawing at him.

Her leg curled around his, bare toes sliding along his jeaned calf. Instinctively, he dropped both hands to the backs of her thighs and lifted her against him, letting her feel the strength and length of his need. She responded by wrapping both legs around his hips. Only the awareness hovering in the back of his mind that his injured son slept mere feet away kept him from shouting approval.

Distance, he thought dimly, just a little more distance. He backed away from the wall, wrapping both arms around her waist and carrying her with him. She reached out with one hand and snagged the edge of the bedroom door, letting him know in no uncertain terms where she wanted him to take her.

He did not disappoint, moving slowly and distractedly over uncertain territory until he found the bed. Turning, he sat down on the edge. Immediately she unwound her legs and went onto her knees astride him. The next moment she pushed him onto his back and followed him down. Her mouth became a wondrous thing, a partner in lavish exploration that left him breathless and craving more. Pushing his hands beneath her shirt, he at last found bare flesh, soft and warm, inexorably feminine, and he wanted to touch every square inch of it.

She felt unexpectedly fragile beneath his hands, from the small span of her waist to the gentle valley of her spine and the flat, smooth planes of her shoulder blades. He even slid a hand up the slender column of her neck and into the silky hair at her nape, marveling at the neatness of her construction. It was the wealth of breast pillowed against his chest that called to him loudest, however, and in order to answer that call he had to lock an arm about her waist and roll her onto her side, dragging them both up a little farther on the bed so that they wound up face to face and more fully upon the mattress.

He now had the freedom to push up her shirt, exposing skin to the faint light drifting through the open doorway, and though it pained him to do so, he broke the intensely pleasurable, constantly renegotiated partnership of their mouths and gently pushed her onto her back in order to feast his eyes on pearly, feminine flesh. Smooth as silk, pale as cream, deliciously warm to the touch, the sight and feel of that bare strip of abdomen moved him in a manner he had not expected. His hand shook as he pushed her shirt higher, revealing the plump globes of her breasts.

Perhaps he had seen finer. The retouched fantasy photos of certain men's magazines always presented perfect breasts, but those photos were unreal and, therefore, unmoving. Nothing and no one had ever evoked in him this feeling of desire heavily laced with reverence. This was not, after all, just any woman beneath his hand. This was Danica. But was she *his* Danica? Suddenly that question was all important. Somehow, not even in this moment was mere sex enough.

He swallowed and found some semblance—a rather husky, rough, faded version—of his normal voice. "I need to know what's going on here, Dani. I need to know what you're feeling, thinking."

"What I'm *feeling*," she said softly, running a hand over his chest, "is that I want you. What I'm *thinking* is that I want you."

Welcome words, but not enough. Gently, he pulled her shirt down, and sat up, drawing up one knee and crossing the other leg beneath it.

"You need to know what I'm feeling and thinking then," he told her. Aware that he was taking a very big chance, he looked down at her face, his heart pounding almost painfully inside his chest. "I'm feeling that I love you, and I'm thinking that one night of making love with you, no matter how much I want it, is not enough."

For a long moment, she displayed no reaction at all. She might have been a statue, a doll, and then her eyelids slowly blinked. The next instant, she sat up, tucked her hair behind one ear, folded her legs and once more lifted her gaze to his. "I have to ask you something," she said. "Maybe I should have asked outright before, but it seemed so disloyal, even unfair, in a way." She sighed and ran a hand through her hair. "At first I was just so consumed with losing her that I couldn't see beyond that, and then I felt so guilty."

"We're talking about Dorinda, aren't we?" he asked, taking her hand in his. At her nod, he rushed to assure her that guilt was misplaced. "Baby, survivor's guilt is a very real phenomenon in cases like this, but, sweetheart, you did nothing to cause your sister's death."

"I urged her to come back here," Danica argued gently, "to settle her business, break her ties and then return with me to Texas. Most especially, I wanted her to break off her relationship with you."

He craned his neck in surprise. "With me? What relationship?"

Danica closed her eyes. "That's what I thought, what I've come to think, rather. You really didn't have a relationship with Dori, did you?"

"A romantic relationship, you mean?"

"Yes."

He lifted a hand to the back of his neck, trying to figure where this was coming from. "Dani, I liked your sister...for the most part. I was even attracted to her on a certain, very elemental level, and I felt sorry for her after Bud was caught stealing, but there was no personal relationship between us of any sort, and there never could be."

"Why not?"

He closed his eyes. That was one question he didn't

want to answer. "Uh, let's just say the negatives out-weighed the positives and leave it at that. Okay?"

She bowed her head and softly said, "I can't, not now. Don't you see? Dori was crazy about you, but now it's *me* who's here with you."

"And that's what you really feel guilty about," he surmised. She nodded almost morosely, and he shook his head, sliding an arm about her shoulders. "Sweet-heart, your sister was a physically beautiful woman, but you are much more to my taste. Yes, I know you were supposedly identical, but where you are soft and sweet, Dorinda was wild and, well, blatant. I would never choose her over you."

"I need you to fully explain why," she pleaded, "why specifically you wouldn't choose her, and I need the truth, Win, all of it."

He pinched the bridge of his nose, hating this and yet wanting to give her what she needed. "It was before Bud's arrest," he told her haltingly, "before anyone had any idea that he was involved in the rus-tling. They'd been coming over for dinner every cou-ple weeks almost from the day they arrived, and Dor-inda was practically a fixture at my mom's coffee table day in and day out. For a while it seemed that I was bumping into her every time I turned around, and frankly it made me uneasy. I mean, she was a married woman, and some of those incidents seemed orchestrated by her."

"What happened?"

He sighed heavily and told her. "One day I walked into my own barn and she was already there, waiting. The next thing I knew, she was all over me and saying that she'd made a mistake with Bud, that she didn't love him, after all, and that she'd rather be with me. I was so shocked I just sort of shoved her away. Then suddenly she was all embarrassed and in tears, and I was so uncomfortable that my skin actually crawled.''

"What did you say to her?"

"I said that I would never get involved with another man's wife. I'd been on the receiving end of that setup, and believe me, it was more than simply humiliating.''

"And then what?" Danica asked.

He felt that uncomfortable creepiness again, but he forthrightly admitted, "Dorinda asked if I would be interested in her if she weren't married, and I hedged by saying that she was a beautiful woman whom few men could resist given the right circumstances. That seemed to satisfy her, and she left.''

Danica bowed her head. "Poor Dori," she whispered.

"I have to tell you that I didn't want to hurt her, but I wasn't feeling real charitable toward her, either," he went on. "I was so shaken that I actually talked over the possibility of visiting family in Jackson Hole for a while just to keep out of her way, but before I could make up my mind about that, Bud got caught trying to transport stolen cattle. Then I did feel sorry for her, even if I was relieved that she was occupied with that whole legal mess, so I just avoided her as best I could, tried to be polite when I couldn't and hoped I wouldn't have to tell her flat out that I could never care for her the way she seemed to want me to. When she left for Texas, I was the most relieved cowboy in Wyoming.''

Danica sighed richly and slumped forward. "When

she came home, all she could talk about, besides how Bud had trashed her life, was you. She made it sound like you two had something going on, and she made it plain that if she came back here to stay she would be coming back to you, or at least *for* you. I was alarmed because a guy who would get involved with a married woman is a poor risk for the long run."

"I couldn't agree more," he said defensively.

"But I didn't know that in the beginning," she confessed. "I only knew what Dori told me. Once she made the decision to come home to Texas for good, we started for here to settle everything. Then the accident..."

"After her death you couldn't bring yourself to question her version."

"There was no reason to," she said, "until a certain cowboy came along and turned everything upside down."

"And now?" he asked softly.

"Now, I'm feeling very sad and very happy at the same time, sad because my sister wasn't the person she should've been, happy because you are so much more than I expected, more than I ever even imagined, especially after Michael."

Intensely gratified, he put his forehead to hers. "Does that mean," he whispered, "that I have reason to hope we might have a future?"

"Oh, yes," she vowed. "If I didn't believe we could have a future, I wouldn't be here in this bed willing to make love with you now."

"To comfort me," he surmised, needing clarification.

She drew back slightly. "Yes, I suppose, because I do care so very much."

"But that's all you're willing to commit to right now, isn't it?" he said.

"I'm just afraid, with everything that's gone on, that it's too soon for me to be sure. I—I guess I haven't learned to trust my own heart yet," she said, "but I want to. You don't know how much I want to."

He pulled in a deep breath. "Then we'll wait," he decided firmly, "and when you decide you're ready, we'll do this again, but you have to know that I'll be asking you to marry me first."

"And I suspect that I'll be saying yes," she whispered, hanging on to his shirt front with both hands. He cupped her cheek with his palm and silently promised to do everything within his power to prove that he was the man for her. Then he moved over, located the pillow and lay down, pulling her down beside him.

"I think I can sleep now," he said, holding her close.

She turned her face into the hollow of his shoulder, her hand gliding up to rest on the side of his neck, and whispered, "I think I can live now, and frankly it wasn't so long ago that I doubted it."

"No doubts," he whispered, closing his eyes. "No doubts for either of us. Soon." Smiling, he allowed sleep to carry them both into the realm of comfort and hope.

Danica surveyed the Thanksgiving table, marveling that it did not collapse beneath the weight of bounty heaped upon it. Madge Champlain's sister, Helen, and her husband had come from Jackson Hole to celebrate the holiday, this being the year their daughter and grandchildren were eating with their son-in-law's family. Helen and Madge were cut from the same cloth when it came to cooking everything in sight. Dani couldn't believe that seven people were expected to eat all this food. She also couldn't believe that the house was toasty warm despite the wind that howled around it or that the ground had been virtually bare this morning after the several feet of snow which had fallen since late September. And yet, here she stood against all odds, one of the seven, warm inside and out, at home in this place of stark landscape and even starker weather, loving these people and this life that she had found here among them.

They had entered into a partnership, after all. Fences had come down and a few new ones had been built to facilitate the movement of cattle, effectively mingling the herds. Hasty preparations had been made for the winter, more for her sake than the Champlains', and she was learning the intricacies of the cattle business in snow country. That and the new clinic which she personally staffed two afternoons a week under the direct guidance of Dr. Sheffield, who came down once a month to see patients, kept her very busy, but not too busy to spend time with Win and Jamesy and Madge and Buck. Somehow, she had been filled by life in this empty land.

"Helen, tell those men to start washing up," Madge said, slicing pickles and arranging them on a relish plate with the tip of her knife. Helen rushed from the room to do that, and Danica smiled at the way Madge fussed with the pickles, as if anyone cared that they were placed just so on the plate. That was Madge, though, always doing just a little more, going that second mile, for everyone around her. It was one of the things Dani loved about her. Madge glanced over her shoulder at Danica then and smiled. "Sugar, you want to start pouring the tea?"

"Sure."

"Isn't it nice to have the family together?" Madge mused as Danica began pouring tea into tumblers.

"It's wonderful," Dani answered. "It's been a long time since I enjoyed this kind of holiday, and frankly, I envy you your family."

Madge slapped the knife down onto the countertop and swung around to face her. "Well, for pity's sake then, jump on board! You must know how we all feel about it, especially Win. He loves you. That's abundantly clear."

"I love him, too," Dani admitted bluntly, "but it isn't quite as simple as jumping on board, you know."

"Does that mean you're going to marry my dad?" Jamesy asked, suddenly appearing at her elbow, his sleeves rolled back from freshly washed hands. The brace was long gone, and the cast on his ankle had come off days earlier.

Danica blinked down at him. "Well, I—I hope so. I'm not quite sure."

"And just what might it take to make you sure?" asked a silky voice close behind her.

She whirled, splashing tea from the pitcher, and nearly bumped into Winston's chest. His hands were parked on his hips. His eyebrows were slightly ele-

vated, his smoky eyes wide on hers, a faint smile
curling at the corners of his mouth. Merciful heaven,
how she loved him!

The past weeks had been the sweetest—and most
frustrating—of her life. The man fairly melted her
with the slightest touch, and he liked to touch *a lot*,
but he'd held firm to his intention not to make love
to her until she married him. She'd made the decision
to do so repeatedly, usually in the throes of passion
so intense that she was certain afterward that he had
fried some part of her brain. It was a decision that
deserved to be made in the calm of reason, however,
and she'd been trying to pick her moment. The problem was that every time they were alone together,
reason was tossed right out the window by desire,
which was anything but calm or reasonable. Perhaps
a family moment was the next best thing. Deliberately, she set down the pitcher and folded her arms.

"Well," she said, "it would help if someone asked
me the proper question."

"Ah." A grin split his handsome face before he
drew his brows together, clasped his hands behind his
back and worried with exaggerated confusion, "And
what might the 'proper question' be, I wonder."

She dropped her arms, stiffening in offense at the
mere idea of his ignorance in this. "You know perfectly well!"

The grin broke out again, and the next thing she
knew, she was being dragged against his chest. "Danica Lynch," he said loudly, locking his arms against
the small of her back, "will you marry me?"

Jamesy jumped up and down, clapping his hands
together anxiously while Danica searched Winston's

eyes, finding everything she'd ever needed there, love and desire and hope and constancy and happiness. "Yes," she answered, never more certain of anything in her life.

He was kissing her before the sound of the word had dissipated into the thin air upon which it rode. Then he was suddenly whirling her around to the accompaniment of applause and laughter from the whole family.

"It's about time, woman!" he exclaimed, setting her on her feet finally. "So pick a day."

"We could do it here!" Madge proposed before Danica could even think about it. "Helen, you can help me decorate the house before you leave." She pointed at Dani then and added, "We can have you right and tight in the fold before Christmas."

"That would make Christmas a real family holiday for us all," Winston added hopefully.

"Yeah, but what about the house?" Buck asked. "I mean, we always planned, Mother and me, to move out once you married. Can't do that on such short order."

"Maybe we could move into Dani's house for awhile," Madge suggested, "just until we can get something built."

"No!" Danica exclaimed. "I don't want you to move out. This is your home."

"Then we'll build something," Winston said quickly. "We could even build onto your cabin, if you want."

"We will not," Dani insisted. "We'll all live right here where we belong!"

"Yoo-hoo!" Jamesy crowed, leaping into the air.

"What sense does it make to gain a family in one moment just to lose half of them the next?" she went on. "This house is big enough for all of us, with room to spare." She looked at Winston then, pleading with her eyes, and played the trump card. "Even with an addition—or two—in the future, we wouldn't be unreasonably crowded."

"Does that mean I'm gonna get a baby brother?" Jamesy demanded excitedly.

"Or sister," Buck said.

"I'd rather have a brother," Jamesy stated emphatically.

"We don't always get to choose," Madge said in a distracted tone.

"But sometimes we do," Winston said softly, smiling down into Danica's eyes.

"Then I choose for all of us to live here from now on," she told him, smiling back.

"I love you," he whispered. "I'll always love you, but thank you for this, anyway." He wrapped his arms around her, folding her close, and she knew that this was right.

"Well, I want a new dining room out of the deal," Madge announced happily. "If the family's getting bigger, the dinner table has to, and that means I need more room."

"Done," Buck announced, slapping his hands together and rubbing them briskly. "Now that that's settled, what're we waiting for? Let's eat."

"Buck Champlain," Madge scolded, teary-eyed, "is your stomach all you can think about at a time like this?"

"What I'm thinking is that we've got plenty to be

thankful for,'' he retorted, ''including all this food.''
He winked at Danica and added, ''Don't you agree,
daughter?''

Suddenly she couldn't speak for the tears clogging
her throat, but she could nod, most emphatically. A
few moments later, gathered around the table, linked
into a circle by the clasp of hands and the willingness
of generous hearts, she smiled at the man next to her
as they bowed their heads. She remembered the
weeks and months of being alone in a barren world
of loss and grief. Those memories would always be
with her, but she would cushion them with happiness
and love, making happier memories her future. Closing her eyes, she thanked God—and a beloved, if im-
perfect, sister—for leading her to love and home.

*   *   *   *   *

Watch for the next exciting book
by beloved Silhouette author
Arlene James
with

HER SECRET AFFAIR

On sale in September 2001
from Silhouette Special Edition.

**You loved
the Maitland
family. Now meet
the long-lost Maitlands...!**

In August 2001, Marie Ferrarella introduces
Rafe Maitland, a rugged rancher with a little girl he'd
do anything to keep, including—*gulp!*—get married,
in **THE INHERITANCE**, a specially packaged story!

Look for it near Silhouette and Harlequin's single titles!

**Then meet Rafe's siblings in
Silhouette Romance® in the coming months:**

Myrna Mackenzie continues the story
of the Maitlands with prodigal
daughter Laura Maitland in
September 2001's
A VERY SPECIAL DELIVERY.

October 2001 brings
the conclusion to this
spin-off of the popular
Maitland family series, reuniting
black sheep Luke Maitland with
his family in Stella Bagwell's
THE MISSING MAITLAND.

Available at your favorite retail outlet.

Where love comes alive™

Visit Silhouette at www.eHarlequin.com   SRMAIT1

Revitalize!

With help from
Silhouette's *New York Times*
bestselling authors
and receive a

FREE

Refresher Kit!

LUCIA IN LOVE by Heather Graham
and **LION ON THE PROWL** by Kasey Michaels

LOVE SONG FOR A RAVEN by Elizabeth Lowell
and **THE FIVE-MINUTE BRIDE** by Leanne Banks

MACKENZIE'S PLEASURE by Linda Howard
and **DEFENDING HIS OWN** by Beverly Barton

DARING MOVES by Linda Lael Miller
and **MARRIAGE ON DEMAND** by Susan Mallery

Don't miss out!

*Look for this exciting promotion, on sale in
October 2001 at your favorite retail outlet.
See inside books for details.*

Only from

Where love comes alive™

Visit Silhouette at www.eHarlequin.com   PSNCP-POP

If you enjoyed what you just read,
then we've got an offer you can't resist!

Take 2 bestselling
love stories FREE!
Plus get a FREE surprise gift!

Clip this page and mail it to Silhouette Reader Service™

IN U.S.A.	IN CANADA
3010 Walden Ave.	P.O. Box 609
P.O. Box 1867	Fort Erie, Ontario
Buffalo, N.Y. 14240-1867	L2A 5X3

YES! Please send me 2 free Silhouette Romance® novels and my free surprise gift. After receiving them, if I don't wish to receive anymore, I can return the shipping statement marked cancel. If I don't cancel, I will receive 6 brand-new novels every month, before they're available in stores! In the U.S.A., bill me at the bargain price of $3.15 plus 25¢ shipping and handling per book and applicable sales tax, if any*. In Canada, bill me at the bargain price of $3.50 plus 25¢ shipping and handling per book and applicable taxes**. That's the complete price and a savings of at least 10% off the cover prices—what a great deal! I understand that accepting the 2 free books and gift places me under no obligation ever to buy any books. I can always return a shipment and cancel at any time. Even if I never buy another book from Silhouette, the 2 free books and gift are mine to keep forever.

215 SEN DFNQ
315 SEN DFNR

Name	(PLEASE PRINT)	
Address	Apt.#	
City	State/Prov.	Zip/Postal Code

 * Terms and prices subject to change without notice. Sales tax applicable in N.Y.
** Canadian residents will be charged applicable provincial taxes and GST.
   All orders subject to approval. Offer limited to one per household and not valid to current Silhouette Romance® subscribers.
   ® are registered trademarks of Harlequin Enterprises Limited.

SROM01   ©1998 Harlequin Enterprises Limited

Feel like a star with Silhouette.

We will fly you and a guest to New York City for an exciting weekend stay at a glamorous 5-star hotel. Experience a refreshing day at one of New York's trendiest spas and have your photo taken by a professional. Plus, receive $1,000 U.S. spending money!

**Flowers...long walks...dinner for two...
how does Silhouette Books
make romance come alive for you?**

Send us a script, with 500 words or less, along with visuals (only drawings, magazine cutouts or photographs or combination thereof). Show us how Silhouette Makes Your Love Come Alive. Be creative and have fun. No purchase necessary. All entries must be clearly marked with your name, address and telephone number. All entries will become property of Silhouette and are not returnable. **Contest closes September 28, 2001.**

Please send your entry to: **Silhouette Makes You a Star!**

In U.S.A.
P.O. Box 9069
Buffalo, NY, 14269-9069

In Canada
P.O. Box 637
Fort Erie, ON, L2A 5X3

Look for contest details on the next page, by visiting www.eHarlequin.com or request a copy by sending a self-addressed envelope to the applicable address above. Contest open to Canadian and U.S. residents who are 18 or over. Void where prohibited.

Our lucky winner's photo will appear in a Silhouette ad. Join the fun!

SRMYAS1

HARLEQUIN "SILHOUETTE MAKES YOU A STAR!" CONTEST 1308
OFFICIAL RULES
NO PURCHASE NECESSARY TO ENTER

1. To enter, follow directions published in the offer to which you are responding. Contest begins June 1, 2001, and ends on September 28, 2001. Entries must be postmarked by September 28, 2001, and received by October 5, 2001. Enter by hand-printing (or typing) on an 8 ½" x 11" piece of paper your name, address (including zip code), contest number/name and attaching a script containing 500 words or less, along with drawings, photographs or magazine cutouts, or combinations thereof (i.e., collage) on no larger than 9" x 12" piece of paper, describing how the Silhouette books make romance come alive for you. Mail via first-class mail to: Harlequin "Silhouette Makes You a Star!" Contest 1308, (in the U.S.) P.O. Box 9069, Buffalo, NY 14269-9069, (in Canada) P.O. Box 637, Fort Erie, Ontario, Canada L2A 5X3. Limit one entry per person, household or organization.

2. Contests will be judged by a panel of members of the Harlequin editorial, marketing and public relations staff. Fifty percent of criteria will be judged against script and fifty percent will be judged against drawing, photographs and/or magazine cutouts. Judging criteria will be based on the following:

    - Sincerity—25%
    - Originality and Creativity—50%
    - Emotionally Compelling—25%

   In the event of a tie, duplicate prizes will be awarded. Decisions of the judges are final.

3. All entries become the property of Torstar Corp. and may be used for future promotional purposes. Entries will not be returned. No responsibility is assumed for lost, late, illegible, incomplete, inaccurate, nondelivered or misdirected mail.

4. Contest open only to residents of the U.S. (except Puerto Rico) and Canada who are 18 years of age or older, and is void wherever prohibited by law; all applicable laws and regulations apply. Any litigation within the Province of Quebec respecting the conduct or organization of a publicity contest may be submitted to the Régie des alcools, des courses et des jeux for a ruling. Any litigation respecting the awarding of a prize may be submitted to the Régie des alcools, des courses et des jeux only for the purpose of helping the parties reach a settlement. Employees and immediate family members of Torstar Corp. and D. L. Blair, Inc., their affiliates, subsidiaries and all other agencies, entities and persons connected with the use, marketing or conduct of this contest are not eligible to enter. Taxes on prizes are the sole responsibility of the winner. Acceptance of any prize offered constitutes permission to use winner's name, photograph or other likeness for the purposes of advertising, trade and promotion on behalf of Torstar Corp., its affiliates and subsidiaries without further compensation to the winner, unless prohibited by law.

5. Winner will be determined no later than November 30, 2001, and will be notified by mail. Winner will be required to sign and return an Affidavit of Eligibility/Release of Liability/Publicity Release form within 15 days after winner notification. Noncompliance within that time period may result in disqualification and an alternative winner may be selected. All travelers must execute a Release of Liability prior to ticketing and must possess required travel documents (e.g., passport, photo ID) where applicable. Trip must be booked by December 31, 2001, and completed within one year of notification. No substitution of prize permitted by winner. Torstar Corp. and D. L. Blair, Inc., their parents, affiliates and subsidiaries are not responsible for errors in printing of contest, entries and/or game pieces. In the event of printing or other errors that may result in unintended prize values or duplication of prizes, all affected game pieces or entries shall be null and void. **Purchase or acceptance of a product offer does not improve your chances of winning.**

6. Prizes: (1) Grand Prize—A 2-night/3-day trip for two (2) to New York City, including round-trip coach air transportation nearest winner's home and hotel accommodations (double occupancy) at The Plaza Hotel, a glamorous afternoon makeover at a trendy New York spa, $1,000 in U.S. spending money and an opportunity to have a professional photo taken and appear in a Silhouette advertisement (approximate retail value: $7,000). (10) Ten Runner-Up Prizes of gift packages (retail value $50 ea.). Prizes consist of only those items listed as part of the prize. Limit one prize per person. Prize is valued in U.S. currency.

7. For the name of the winner (available after December 31, 2001) send a self-addressed, stamped envelope to: Harlequin "Silhouette Makes You a Star!" Contest 1197 Winners, P.O. Box 4200 Blair, NE 68009-4200 or you may access the www.eHarlequin.com Web site through February 28, 2002.

Contest sponsored by Torstar Corp., P.O. Box 9042, Buffalo, NY 14269-9042.

SRMYAS2

Warning: Fairy tales do come true!

SILHOUETTE *Romance*

brings you an irresistible new series

The Cinderella Conspiracy

by Lilian Darcy

The three Brown sisters don't believe in
happily-ever-afters—until each one is rescued
by her own gallant knight!

September 2001
Cinderella After Midnight—SR #1542

November 2001
Saving Cinderella—SR #1555

January 2002—
Finding Her Prince—SR #1567

Available at your favorite retail outlet.

Silhouette®
Where love comes alive™

Visit Silhouette at www.eHarlequin.com   SRCIN